GUNNAR'S GUARDIAN

BY

PANDORA PINE

Gunnar's Guardian

Copyright © Pandora Pine 2020

All Rights Reserved

First Digital Edition: May 2020

PROLOGUE

Kennedy

June, 2000…

Tiago had finally gone too far. I was sitting in the center of what used to be the living room with blood dripping down my chin and my left eye swollen to the point that I could no longer see out of it. There wasn't much to see anyway. Not anymore.

Furniture was overturned and the glass coffee table was shattered. Wicked shards of glass littered the living room rug, twinkling like stars in the glow of the television. There was blood on some of the broken pieces. It had been my mother who'd broken the glass. Tiago's right hook to the face sent her sprawling. She'd gotten her right forearm in front of her face a spilt-second before it hit the glass.

I'd seen the fear in Tiago's eyes when he grabbed my bleeding mother and dragged her toward the bedroom they shared. She'd gone kicking and screaming, knocking a lamp and the end table over in the process. The table tipped onto its top, leaving the legs sticking up like a beetle on its back. I could see the blood trail she'd left as he'd hustled her off.

The fight had started over homework. My mother asked me to get working on it. I said no. There were ten minutes left in *Buffy the Vampire Slayer* and I was mad for Spike. He made my heart pound in my chest and gave me a funny feeling in the pit of my stomach that I couldn't explain, but wanted more of.

Tiago hit me for daring to say no to the order. For once, my mother stepped in between the two of us and she'd gotten hit so hard that the glass-topped table had broken her fall and probably her arm.

Ten minutes ago, life was normal. Well, as normal as things were in this place. My mom had known Tiago for a week before letting him move in with us. That had been almost six months ago. Being fast on her feet with men was her usual way. Kitty Lynch was *never* without a man.

My real father was dead. Lost at sea in a fishing accident. That was life in New Bedford, Massachusetts. When the fleet left the harbor, there was no guarantee any of them would come home.

It was always the same when my mom moved in a new boyfriend. The men were nice to me for the first day or two. Then shit hit the fan. I was slapped. Beaten. Burned with cigarettes. One asshole even tried to touch me down *there*, but I wasn't having any of that. I punched him in the junk and then he punched me in the face. I woke up three days later in the hospital, but at least he was gone. The house didn't stay empty of a man for long.

Rinse. Repeat. Second verse, same as the first.

Loud cries from the back of the house brought me back to the present. It was my mother screaming for help.

"No, Tiago! Don't! Stop! Noooooooooo!" My mother's cry ended on what sounds to me like a gurgle. Even at ten years old, I knew what that sound meant. I was an orphan. If I didn't move and move fast, Tiago would kill me too.

I wobbled to my feet, my brain scrambling for a place to hide. In a two-bedroom apartment, there weren't many places a kid my size could go. The broom closet was my only option. I looked longingly at the front door but knew that other people would get hurt if I dragged neighbors into our fight. This was my fault. I needed to deal with it like a man.

Stumbling, I moved toward the kitchen. That's when all hell broke loose. Tiago bellowed from the bedroom. His rampaging footfalls were getting closer and closer. "I'll kill you too! You motherfucking bastard!"

Frozen. Just like a deer in the headlights. I couldn't move. Couldn't breathe. This was how my life was going to end. Maybe now I'd get to meet my father for the first time. My eyes slipped shut as I prayed for my end to be quick and painless.

Tiago roared again. This time he was closer. My eyes flew open and I saw the knife. It was shining from the reflection of the bare kitchen bulb. My mother's blood formed pregnant droplets at the tip before slowly falling to the floor. It reminded me of the opening to CSI.

I wasn't supposed to watch that show, but on nights when Tiago was passed out drunk, I'd sneak into the living room and watch it. Gil Grissom and his team were heroes. They'd help a kid like me. If they knew I existed. If *they* actually existed.

The blade rose again. I knew if I didn't do something to defend myself it would be my blood mixed with hers on the blade of that kitchen knife. I backed away from Tiago as he advanced toward me. My right leg bumped against something. It was the chair he sat in for meals. Grabbing it, I threw it toward him. Tiago had been charging at me so hard that the chair only bounced off his hip, skittering into what was left of the living room.

I was exposed. There was nowhere else to run. Tiago tightened his grip on the blade. I backed into the kitchen sink. There were no dirty dishes in it. Nor were there clean dishes drying in the rack. That was one of Tiago's rules. There was nothing to use against him. No weapons. I was trapped. I did the only thing I could do. "Hail Mary, full of grace..."

As if my small prayer worked, the front door to the apartment splintered open. There were shouts of "POLICE!" Officers with guns drawn swarmed the room and then Tiago. One of them grabbed me, pulling me to the side. Asked if I was all right. My mother was dead. I was bleeding and could only see out of one eye. No, I was not all right.

A neighbor must have called the cops. Probably Mrs. Simonson from next door. She was a sweet old woman, but always had her nose in everyone else's business. Her gossiping ways may have saved my life that night. I was never able to thank her.

Everything happened at light speed after that. Tiago was arrested and taken out of the apartment. They brought my mother out next. She was on a gurney the EMTs brought into the apartment and zipped into a black bag that looked like it should be holding suits, not a human being. Not my mother. I wasn't able to say goodbye. The officer watching over me said they couldn't afford to have me contaminate the scene. Gil Grissom would have told me the same thing.

On television I would have had this dramatic last scene with my mother. I'd vow to never sleep until her killer was brought to justice. Later on in the episode there would be bitter and cutting lines I would deliver to Tiago when I finally faced him. He'd pay for what he'd done.

None of those things happened. The officer, Garcia, her name was, brought me back to my room, which had survived the confrontation undamaged. She'd told me to pack my things and handed me a black plastic garbage bag.

I stuffed all my clean clothes into the bag, along with Baxter, a worn teddy bear my mother had gotten me for Christmas two years ago. I knew I was going to have to be a man now, but this bear was the only thing I had left of her. The last thing that went into the bag was a picture of the two of us together, sitting on the couch. Before Tiago. Before everything went to hell.

Officer Garcia walked me out of the apartment for what I knew would be the last time. I didn't bother to turn back. There was nothing there I wanted to remember.

A woman from Child Protective Services was waiting outside. The dark neighborhood was illuminated with blue and white police lights bouncing around in concert with the red lights from the ambulance. There was no need for it to hurry away. Nothing could be done for my mother now.

I was introduced to the CPS worker. Her name was Patricia, but she insisted I call her Patti. She got me seated in her car before stuffing my things into the trunk. It was fitting everything I owned in the world was in a garbage bag. This had been a garbage life. Like attracts like, as my mother used to say. I never understood what she'd meant, until that moment.

Patti pulled the car away from the curb and started chattering to me about the weather and something called Gloucester. I had no idea what a Gloucester was, so I shut my eyes and thought of Buffy and Spike. Unbelievably, I felt myself drift off to sleep.

A car door shutting startled me awake. It took a moment for me to remember where I was. Then it came to me. Tiago had murdered my mother. I was in some social worker's car.

The driver's side backdoor opened, and Patti reached for me. I managed to get my seatbelt off and climb out of the car. What I saw surprised me. I figured I was bound for some orphanage, but instead I was in a neighborhood with houses. A family was standing in the driveway with smiles on their faces.

"I'm Mandy McCoy and this is my husband, David." The woman looked like she was in her late thirties, but it was hard to tell in the dark. She was blonde with blue or green eyes, slender and wearing an ugly floral print bathrobe that went all the way to her toes. Mandy was older than my mother. My heart pinched as my mind supplied the image of her in a body bag being wheeled out of our shitty apartment.

David was tall, probably over six feet. His sandy blond hair was sticking up in the back and his bathrobe wasn't tied. The belt hung down his long legs. He wore glasses and a kind smile I knew was filled with pity.

"Hi," I managed to say. It sounded more like a squeak. To say I was scared was an understatement. Who were these people? What was I doing here?

"These are our sons Ozzy, Dallas, and Hennessey." She pointed to the three young boys who were huddled around David.

I took my time studying the kids. Ozzy was tall and skinny with a wicked scar running down the side of his left cheek. He looked mean. Dallas wore a brave smile. It was obvious he was terrified of something. Maybe me. Hennessy had longish dirty blond hair. He stood there with his arms crossed over his thin chest, looking like he was pissed at something. Probably me.

One of these things didn't look like the others. It was obvious Hennessey was Mandy's real son. Ozzy, with his jet-black hair, and Dallas, with his flaming red locks, didn't look anything like Mandy or David.

"This is going to be your new home, Kennedy," Patti said. "Mandy and David are going to be your foster parents."

Oh. That explained why Ozzy and Dallas didn't look like the McCoys or each other. They were *foster* kids. Shit, if they were foster kids, that meant I was too. My heart sunk even further.

It was too much. Even though I was a man now, I started to cry.

Mandy rushed to my side. Kneeling in front of me she put a hand on my shoulder. "It's going to be all right. You're safe here. Safe. Nothing bad is going to happen to you. I promise." She smiled at me through tears of her own. "You're going to be all right."

Nothing would ever be all right again.

1

Kennedy

June 2020…

It had been a long-ass shift. Making matters worse, was the fact that it wasn't even my shift to take. Anders March had banged in sick and I was the dumbass who agreed to take his patrol car for him on the Charlie shift, 10:00 p.m. until 7:00 a.m., on a night when lunacy was par for the course.

Christ, I've never been much of a martyr, but here I was, Detective Kennedy Lynch, on patrol. Adding insult to injury was the fact that I had to be in my blues, instead of dressed in jeans and a wife-beater, my usual attire when I was roaming the streets as a member of the Vice Squad. Hookers and blow were my jam. So to speak.

Last night had been the first night of the full Strawberry Moon. Who the fuck was it who named these damned moons? Whoever it was should have their head examined. Sweet, succulent strawberries had *nothing* in common with the lunatic madness brought on by the full moon.

The only thing *worse* than a full moon was a full *blood* moon in the heat of summer. It was only the second week in June, but Gloucester, Massachusetts had been above ninety degrees for the last week or so, with no sign of relief in sight.

The "blood" moon had certainly lived up to its name. There had been two stabbings, a shooting, and some kind of dust up between rival drug gangs, who'd thankfully decided to use their fists instead of bullets and blades. I'd spent more time in the ER at Gloucester Memorial Hospital tonight than I had in the last month.

What I wanted to do more than anything was peel this sweaty, stinking uniform off my body, take a cool shower, and then a nap in my bedroom with the air conditioner set to deep freeze. At that temperature, it was too cold for penguins. My second shift of the day started at 3:00 p.m. At least then I'd be back in my usual uniform. My second skin.

Turning onto my street, I knew my dreams of a nap were not to be. Sitting in front of the townhouse next to mine was a small U-Haul truck and one teenager perched on the loading ramp looking sulky. The minute he saw my Gloucester Police SUV, he bolted from the ramp, running to the driver's side of the truck.

What the fuck was up with this guy? My cop radar was on high alert, until I parked the car in my driveway and shut off the ignition. I heard the dying strains of some hip-hop bullshit playing loud enough to rupture my eardrums before the sound was turned off. The kid must have thought I was here on a noise complaint.

"Sorry, Officer," the kid muttered with a too-bright smile. He never made eye contact before quickly ducking into the back of the truck.

It didn't hit me until he walked into the back of the U-Haul and came out with a suitcase, that this guy was my new neighbor. The end unit next to my townhouse had been for sale since the week before Christmas. My retired neighbors were off to spend their golden years in the Sunshine State. The house had been empty, but for a few open houses, since then.

Motherfucking *fuck*. The last thing I needed was some kid living next door having loud, obnoxious parties with his loud, obnoxious friends. A deep frown furrowed my face.

"Shit, you're not here to arrest me, are you, *officer*?" The last word was sneered like it tasted bad in his mouth. He stood with his hands on his slim hips and an incredulous look in his startling green eyes.

The kid was a string-bean. He stood about five foot, eight inches and looked like he needed a sandwich. Maybe more than one. I couldn't decide if his flaming red hair or his emerald green eyes were his best feature. It sure as hell wasn't his smart mouth with its full lips. His attire consisted of baggy jeans and a Pink Floyd concert tee. Unless he'd gone as a toddler, there was no way this kid had attended a Pink Floyd show. The thought of that alone got under my skin.

With those words, I was back in cop-mode. Who did this kid think he was, acting like this? "I'll give you one opportunity to adjust your own attitude before I do it for you. If I were here to arrest you, you'd already be in cuffs." I paused, caught in the glitter of his hard, green eyes. "I'm your neighbor, dumbass." It wasn't how I'd planned to end my tirade, but if I'd gotten much closer to the snot-nosed brat I wouldn't have been be able to keep my hands off him.

Instead of backing down, I could see my words lit a fire in the kid, who wasn't actually a kid. Once I was standing nearly toe to toe with him, I could see he was in his early twenties. "Adjust *my* attitude? Check your own, *Boomer*!" He scoffed openly at me.

Boomer? How the hell old did this kid think I was? Up until that moment, I'd thought I looked a bit younger than my thirty years. That wasn't the point. Or was it? The little bastard was just trying to goad me. "I'm not the one with the attitude here, *son*." I drew out that last word. My hands were fisted on my hips and I was using every inch of my 6'3" frame to tower over him.

"I'm not your son, asshole!" He shouted. His voice echoing in the box truck. The anger in his voice was real. So was the hurt in his eyes. "I'm no one's son," he muttered to himself.

What the hell did that mean? Had his father died? Disowned him? Kicked him out? I took a step back, waiting for my training to kick in. "Look, I'm sorry. We seem to have gotten off on the wrong foot." I took a deep breath, all the while watching his body language. The anger had drained from his eyes, replaced by sadness and something else. Maybe confusion. His body was coiled and ready to strike. His hands were still balled into fists.

"Wrong foot, my ass." There wasn't as much heat behind his words.

"I'm Detective Kennedy Lynch. I work for the Gloucester Police Department." The department was big on community policing, so I figured I should do what I could to leave him with a favorable opinion of the department.

"*Detective*?" he snorted. "So why the hell do you look like you spent the morning directing traffic?" A devious smile curved his lips.

I could feel my anger start to roil in my gut again. There was no way I was going to rise to this kid's bait. "It's called sacrifice. Some asshole called out sick. He works patrol. Instead of getting a good night's sleep before my actual shift starts, I took someone else's so that your delicate ass could sleep peacefully last night." I didn't know why I felt the need to explain myself to this amoeba. He looked like the kind of kid who had never heard the word sacrifice before, let alone tried it on for size.

"Uh, huh," the kid half-grunted.

The only reason I was still standing here instead of being in a nice cool shower was because, like it or not, this guy was my neighbor. We were going to be stuck together, so to speak. "Good to meet you." I turned to head down my driveway. His voice stopped me.

"Gunnar Prince. It's good to meet you." The kid held out his hand in what I knew was a half-hearted gesture.

Prince? Jesus, Mary, and Joseph. If ever a kid lived up to a last name, this was it. There was a regal air about him. Rarified. As if his shit didn't stink. At that point, I didn't have the energy to tell him otherwise. "Good to meet you too." I took a deep breath and reached out for his slender hand. It had been my intention to give him a quick, hard pump. The kid obviously hadn't been taught how to shake like a man, or if he had, he'd forgotten. His wrist was limper than week old lettuce.

When our palms slid together, every thought of teaching the kid a lesson flew from my mind. My entire body tensed, with my gut feeling like it was in free-fall. Fuck. Fuck. *Fuck.* There was no way I could be attracted to this bratty boy. I was tired after working a long shift, not to mention annoyed over not already being in bed. It was hot as fuck out here and holding the kid's–Gunnar's–hand wasn't helping matters.

Gunnar pulled away as if he'd been burned. He stared at the palm of his hand for a few seconds. I couldn't help but wonder if he was looking to see if his skin had been singed.

I may have been out of the dating game for a while, but I knew when a man was attracted to me. It was bad enough that I wanted to bend him over the moving truck's ramp and fuck him into the next county, but adding in the very obvious fact that he would let me, was enough to send me running for the hills. That was it. I was out. Not just out, but *out*. "Good to meet you. Gotta run. Need to grab a nap in the A/C before my next shift starts. Keep the music down." I started to walk away, knowing that every second I stood near him was one second closer to me making my raunchy fantasy come true. It was Gunnar's parting shot that stopped me cold.

"There's no electricity, *Dad*." His words were followed by an eyeroll that looked like it hurt.

"What the hell do you mean there's *no* electricity?" It was a bright sunny day, so there was no streetlights on and I couldn't see lights on in my neighbors' houses. Come to think of it, I didn't hear the mechanical roar of air conditioners. Shiiiit. Instead of a nap in the deep freeze, it looked like I was going to be sweating my balls off.

My shoulders slumping in obvious defeat, I headed back toward my house, pulling my keys from my pocket. With every step toward my front door, I felt absolute exhaustion creeping over my entire body.

After I let myself into the house, I flipped the living room light switch out of habit. I was shocked when the room lit up. Why the hell would Gunnar say there was no electricity?

A moment later it hit me. I burst out laughing so hard that I needed to brace an arm against the back of a chair. The electricity wasn't out, Gunnar hadn't bothered to call the utility to have it turned on.

Dumbass...

2

Gunnar

Ten minutes after Kennedy let himself into his house, my hand was still tingling. I kept looking down at my palm, thinking there would be *something* there. Some residue that the rude-ass cop left behind. Not only could I feel the ghost of his touch, but my cock had woken up and taken notice of my burly neighbor.

Officer Asshole wasn't bad looking for an *older* man. He stood well over six feet tall. He was stacked, but not bursting out of his uniform like some 'roided out dickhead. His dirty blond hair was cut short. It looked to me like his usual style was a crewcut that had gotten to the shaggy stage. Kennedy's eyes, though, they were the most vivid blue I'd ever seen. They reminded me of the Mediterranean after a storm. My dick twitched at the thought of those eyes staring up at me while he sucked me off.

Shit, I needed to stop this train of thought before it left the station. It was my cock that had gotten me into this mess. Now I was lost, with no idea how to find my way back and no plan on how to move forward. Not that it mattered. I could never go home again. I should have known better. I should have *done* better, but that was all water under the bridge now.

I'm gay. It took me a long time to admit it to myself. Much longer still to say the words out loud to someone else. There had been hints along the way. School friends that made my heart beat faster. Teachers I couldn't take my eyes off of. I'd still been unsure about who I was and all that, when I saw Drew Brees in a tight pair of football pants. There was no way I could deny who I was any longer. I wanted him in a way that kept my dick perpetually hard. That ass sealed my fate in more ways than one.

My father, August Prince, owns a chain of successful car dealerships in Rockport, Gloucester, and Manchester-by-the-Sea. He wasn't selling rust bucket Chevys or Fords. No, his stable included BMW, Mercedes, Porsche, and Infinity. High-end cars for high-end people, as he was fond of saying.

I was supposed to be the heir to his kingdom. Pun *intended*. The last thing I wanted was my entire life mapped out for me. It's what I got though. Four years at Boston University, then I would have been off to Harvard Business School *if* I hadn't fucked everything up.

My grades had never been the best. I hated every second of what I was studying. It was like a switch flipped in my head against being a business major. I did what I had to do to get by. At first. My grades got worse as freshman turned to sophomore year and so on.

I screwed the pooch senior year. Looking back now, I regret tanking the final semester on purpose. I never attended one lecture. Never handed in a paper or took an exam. BU expelled me. Told me, in so many words, that I wouldn't be allowed to return under any circumstance. They wanted their spots filled by students who were there to learn, not pooch screw.

Predictably enough, my father went nuclear. Called me every name in the book. Moron. Fuck up. Shit heap. And those were the tamer ones. Things still would have been okay if I'd let it end there. I didn't.

Out of all the things I'd done to fuck up my life, the one thing my father couldn't or *wouldn't* get past was the fact that I am gay. No son of mine is going to be a _____. Fill in the blank with the gay slur of the week.

After the dust started to settle over my being expelled from college, I was feeling antsy, caged in. One night when my parents were out to dinner, I invited over some company. *Male* company. He was fucking me so hard that the headboard of my king-sized bed was knocking into the wall behind it. I was having the time of my life until my parents burst into the room and caught me with my legs up in the air as I urged my partner to, "fuck me like he meant it."

It turned out my mother wasn't feeling well, so they'd ended their night early. When they'd come into the house, they'd heard the bed knocking against the wall and thought it meant I was in trouble. I was, but only after I'd been caught.

My father wanted me out of the house the second I had my pants back on. He's a real prince among men. Pun *definitely* intended. My mother stood by and watched with her lips zipped. I grabbed what would fit in my school backpack and was out the door.

I'd spent the last month crashing on friends' couches, wearing out my welcome, friend by friend. Just when I was down to my last sofa, I'd gotten a text from my father. It hadn't been much, just one line, "Your things are in the driveway."

Hence the U-Haul. I'd been in for a bit of a surprise when I'd gotten home. Three suitcases and a couple of boxes filled with toiletries were sitting in the driveway. There was no furniture. No 65" plasma television. No sound system. Not even my fucking alarm clock.

Mavis, our live-in cook, had been the one to meet me in the driveway. She'd been more of a mother to me than Athena Prince had ever been. It was Mavis who soothed my fears, bandaged my cuts, and was there for me in the middle of the night when I needed someone to talk to.

While I did my best to hold back my anger, she explained what was going on. Mavis told me the old man only wanted me to have the clothes on my back. She'd managed to get him to agree to letting her pack whatever would fit into my suitcases.

At that point, I was grateful to have my clothes, but the only place I had to keep them was in my Dodge Charger, which was thankfully paid off. If it wasn't, I had a feeling my father would have insisted on keeping it too.

I'd been trying to figure out what my next move was when Mavis held out a medium-sized manila envelope. It had my name on it in my mother's handwriting. Not expecting much, I'd torn it open. Two things tumbled out: a letter in her elegant scrawl and a stack of cash.

The letter explained the cash was from money she'd been squirreling away from her weekly allowance. There were three separate admonitions not to spend it too quickly or frivolously. This was all I was going to get from either of them. It was time to make my own way in this world.

Thankfully, the last couch I was sleeping on belonged to Bryce Hopkinton. I'd been friends with his son, Randal, since kindergarten. Bryce was a property manager who had several homes available to rent. I picked the townhouse next to Kennedy's because it was the cheapest thing he had. The cash from my mother amounted to a little under ten thousand dollars. I didn't know how long I'd be living off it. I didn't know anything right now.

A bolt of thunder startled me out of my thoughts. While I'd been reliving my greatest hits, a storm had moved in. One drop of rain hit my face. It was quickly followed by another and another. Before I could move, it was pouring and I was soaked to the skin.

I was wrong when I said I didn't know anything. I knew I was wet. And miserable.

3

Kennedy

Even at half past one on a Monday afternoon, my brother Hennessey's bar, Bait, was hopping. It was mostly known around town as a cop bar, but anyone was welcome. I shouldered my way through the crowd to the table at the back, next to the kitchen. Two familiar faces were waiting for me, my brothers, Ozzy and Dallas. Both were dressed for work, Ozzy in his Gloucester fire department uniform and Dallas in the emergency services uniform he wore as an EMT.

"Where's Hen?" Turning around in a slow circle, I didn't see our other brother anywhere.

"He's in the back dealing with some issue with this week's tequila delivery." Ozzy ran an absent finger along the edge of the wicked scar that started near his left ear and ended a few centimeters shy of his mouth. I knew instantly there was something up with him. Now wasn't the time to bring it up.

"Christ! I order the same shit every week. Why do they have such a hard time getting it fucking right?" Hennessey sat down hard in the seat next to me. His long blonde hair was piled atop his head in a messy man bun. He was a handsome guy, but the hairstyle in combination with his scruffy beard did nothing for him.

"Did you figure it out?" Dallas asked. He took a sip from the Mountain Dew in front of him. It was all Dallas drank, during the day, anyway. I never understood it. That shit looks and tastes like warm piss. Not that I would know what *that* tastes like, but it sucked, regardless.

Hennessey rolled his icy blue eyes. "Come in tonight, I'll be debuting a new tequila." He threw a careless hand in the air. "Whatever." He turned to me. "What the fuck is wrong with you? You look like shit." A bright smile lit up his grumpy face. Nothing made my brother happier than giving me the business.

"I worked a patrol shift last night." I signaled the bartender for a black coffee. I was going to need something to keep going.

"Jesus, I heard it was busy. Full moon brings out all the crazies." Ozzy shook his head. He'd stopped touching his scar and was checking me over like Hennessey had done earlier. Say what I would about my brothers, they *always* had my back.

"I spent half my shift in the ER getting two rival street gangs treated for cuts and broken bones and that wasn't even the *craziest* part of my day." Shit, I should have kept my mouth shut. I was so damned tired. I hadn't been able to sleep at all after my impromptu meeting with Gunnar. I did manage to jerk off, so that was something, I supposed.

The bartender set my coffee down in front of me. It was ninety-seven degrees in Gloucester with no hint of the usual sea breeze. What the hell had I been thinking ordering something hot to drink? Maybe I was losing my mind?

Hennessey's light eyebrows shot high. He could sense my distress. His icy eyes lit up like a kid at Christmas. "You met someone, didn't you?"

"Of course I didn't meet *someone*. What the hell are you talking about?" I did meet someone though, but not the kind of *someone* Hennessey was hinting at.

"Come on, man. Spill it. I can see it in your eyes." Dallas batted his long red lashes at me. "We're going to get it out of you one way or the other. Why not make it easy on yourself?"

As much as I hated to admit it, Dallas had a point. They would get it out of me one way or another. By any means necessary, if I knew Hennessey. I sighed dramatically making them think they were really twisting my arm here. "When I got off shift this morning all I wanted to do was sleep for a couple of hours before I had to go back into work. When I got home, there was a U-Haul truck being unloaded by some kid." I mentally crossed my fingers, hoping that explanation would be enough to throw them off the trail.

"Kid?" Ozzy grimaced.

"Jesus Christ, sicko! He wasn't *that* young. At first, I thought he was like seventeen or eighteen years old, but after listening to his tale of woe I'd guess he's about twenty or twenty-one." Not that I cared.

Ozzy started to laugh. Motherfucker. My brother knew I hadn't been talking about some ten-year-old kid, he just used that as an excuse to get me to spill my guts. And it worked.

"I don't understand," there was a gleam in Hennessey's blue eyes. Oh, he understood all right. "How did this *boy* keep you from grabbing any sleep?" His eyes opened even wider. "You fucked him, didn't you? In the U-Haul?" He was rubbing his hands together as if he were about to hear something juicy.

"No! I didn't fuck him." I sure as hell wasn't about to tell them that I'd *wanted* to. Badly. "He's as dumb as they come. Fucking millennials. Kid didn't even know he had to call the electric company to have the juice turned on." Okay, that was a little mean. At least I'd gone over and explained the situation to him. The temperature would be back up in the high nineties that afternoon and no one deserved to battle the heat out with no air conditioning or refrigeration. It'd been my one good deed for the day. Gunnar didn't even thank me. Little fucker. Although, to be honest, I don't think he believed me at first.

"I suppose you brought him over to your house and cooled him down." Ozzy fanned his face for emphasis.

"Christ, no! I gave him the number for the electric company and went back home." With a raging hard on. Gunnar had opened the door wearing only boxer shorts. I'd said what I needed to say and practically ran from the place, guaranteeing I kept my hands to myself. They were on my cock the second the door was shut and locked behind me, make no mistake about that.

"I know these kids don't have the brain God gave an ant, but how the hell *didn't* he know you needed to have the electricity turned on?" Ozzy wore a puzzled look on his face, causing his scar to twist even more gruesomely against his face.

"Let's just say this kid wasn't raised with a silver spoon in his mouth. It was platinum, studded with diamonds." I had done a little bit of research on Gunnar Prince once my ravenous dick had been satisfied.

"You live on a nice middle-class street and all, but what the hell is a kid with *that* kind of money doing moving into your neighborhood?" Dallas turned to Ozzy, and then Hennessey, for an answer to his question when all I could do was shrug my shoulders.

"His name is Gunnar Prince. Apparently, he is, or *was*, the heir to the Prince family dynasty of car dealerships. I don't know any details, but it seemed like the two of them were most definitely on the outs." Gunnar had muttered that he was no one's son. If that didn't scream family troubles, I don't know what did.

"His father is the douche on television telling people how simple it is to drive away in a new Mercedes?" A grimace twisted Dallas's lips. "Sure, I can afford a Mercedes on an EMT's salary. I'd have to live in the damn thing, but I can *afford* one." Dallas rolled his green eyes. "Kid must be a chip off the old block." Dallas looked as if that didn't make Gunnar worth much of anything in his eyes.

For some reason Dallas's attitude lit a fire in my belly. "I think something bad happened to him. I'm guessing he came out and things went south from there."

Dallas leaned in closer. The superior look was gone, replaced by one of concern. "You think the old man gave him the boot for being gay?"

"I don't know. The kid didn't seem to be in much of a mood to talk. We both rubbed each other the wrong way." That was the understatement of the century. "He called me a fucking Boomer, for Christ's sake." That comment, more than anything else he'd said, pissed me off the most.

Ozzy slapped a meaty hand on my shoulder. "Don't feel bad, old man. Those kids think anyone older than thirty is ancient."

I threw his hand off me. "I am older than thirty." Only by a few months, but that wasn't the point. "Asshole." Maybe it wasn't Gunnar Prince. Maybe everyone was just rubbing me the wrong way today.

"Okay, so you didn't fuck this rich bitch. What's got you so riled up?" Hennessey wore a serious look on his face. He wasn't messing with me this time, it was a real question.

"I don't know." It was the damnedest thing. I really *didn't* know. My heart pounded like I'd run a marathon and my skin had tingled all over when we shook hands. The only explanation for that was my being attracted to him. Which really was ridiculous. I had to be at least ten years older than him and judging by the way he spoke to me, he wasn't interested in some broken-down traffic cop. Which I most definitely was *not*.

"He obviously found some way to get under your skin," Ozzy chimed in.

"Yeah." Picking up my coffee, I slammed it back in a few swallows. I was done talking about this. I wasn't the kind of guy who sat around talking about my feelings, even with my brothers. "I'm off. Gotta get to the station and get ready for my shift."

Ozzy stood up with him. "Same here. It's been two days since The Scorcher last struck. I want to go over the fire again in case there's something I'm missing."

In addition to there being all sorts of craziness going on thanks to the full moon, Ozzy and the rest of the Gloucester Police Department had been dealing with a firebug. The blazes had been happening every couple of days or so for the last three weeks. "Let me know if you want me to take a look at your file. Sometimes it helps having a fresh pair of eyes." I had a feeling the arsonist was the reason for Ozzy's earlier upset.

My brother opened the door for me, and I was immediately hit by a wall of heat. It wasn't that I minded the warm weather so much, but this many days in a row of ninety degree plus temperatures? It was enough to make anyone snap.

"What if I can't catch him?" Ozzy's dark eyes flitted back and forth between the sidewalk, his car, and my feet.

My first impression of Osborne Graves had been that he was an angry kid who was mad at the entire world. The fact that there was now one extra body in the foster home he'd been living in wasn't helping his disposition. It turned out my first impression of him was wrong. He'd been a serious boy at twelve years old. Now, twenty years later, that much was still true. He also had a heart of gold.

"You *will* catch him." It sounded like lip service, but Ozzy knew he could trust me. He was something of a prodigy in the fire department. He passed the entrance exam with flying colors the day after he turned eighteen and had spent the last fourteen years working his way up through the ranks of the department. At thirty-one years old, he was the youngest fire captain in the history of the Gloucester Fire Department and was the second youngest in the state of Massachusetts. Some guy out near Worcester beat him by a matter of sixty-four days.

"There's something here I'm missing. I'm sure of it." Ozzy gave his head a shake. His hands were bunched into fists at his side.

"I've got an hour before my shift starts. I'll come back to the firehouse with you." Truth be told I had a shitload of my own work waiting for me on my desk. It would keep. Ozzy was more important than a bunch of reports.

Family was everything.

4

Gunnar

I had never felt more stupid in my entire life. Not only was there no electricity turned on in the house, the same went for natural gas, which apparently fueled my stove and the dryer.

Hearing the news from Kennedy Lynch, of *all* people, had only pissed me off more. I always managed to make myself look like a fucking idiot in front of the older man. I knew when he looked at me all he saw was some stupid kid. What I couldn't admit to him, but could admit to myself, was that he was right.

I'd never given a second thought about what it would take to live in this house I was renting. I guess part of me assumed everything would be done for me just like it always had been at home. I didn't think it was possible to be any more naïve than I already was, but then I'd realized there was no food in the house.

At the local supermarket I'd been tempted to pick up TV dinners and frozen pizza, but now that I was a man out on my own, I figured it was time that I start acting like one. For the first time in my life, I walked through the meat and produce sections of the grocery store. I grabbed the fixings to make salad and some premade hamburgers. How hard could it possibly be to cook up a burger? The people at McDonald's did it every day. There was no reason at all I couldn't do it at home.

Of course, the realization that I could cook a meal for myself at home brought me to the next realization: with what? There was nothing in the house for me to cook with, or to eat off. My trip to the grocery store was followed up with a quick trip to Target to buy the essentials: plates, silverware, and a ginormous box of pots and pans. If I didn't watch myself, I was going to burn through the money my mother had left me. And then what? I truly would be living out of my car. I might have been nothing but a smart ass for the first twenty-one years of my life, but starting today I was just going to be smart.

I'd been on cloud nine when I got home. The house had cooled off nicely while I'd been gone, thanks to Kennedy leaving me with the phone number to the electric company. I really did owe him big time for what he did for me today. I'd been a bit of a dick when he'd come over to explain about the electricity.

It had still been raining cats and dogs when he'd come over to knock on my door. He'd changed out of his tightfitting police uniform and had been dressed in a tight white T-shirt and a pair of shorts. He was soaked to the skin, which made his white T-shirt mold perfectly to every muscle. Boomer or not, the man was a work of art.

Giving my head a little shake, I'd gotten down to the business of unpacking my purchases. It turned out the one thing I forgot to buy at the supermarket was dish soap and some kind of scrubby. I supposed it didn't much matter, at the moment. I could leave my dirty dishes in the sink and go out again tomorrow morning. It had been a long-ass day, and all I wanted to do was eat something.

Twenty minutes later, I was feeling rather proud of myself. All of the dishes and pots and pans had been put away but for the small frying pan I would need for my burger. I tore open the cellophane package holding the patties, and dumped cooking oil in before throwing one of the burgers into the pan. Turning the heat up to high, I went about making my salad.

The house was so quiet. More than anything, I'd wanted to go out and buy myself a television, but with my financial situation in dire straits, I couldn't afford one. Thankfully my phone was paid up for the next month and I would be able to stream anything I wanted. It was going to stink watching it on such a tiny screen, but I would suck it up for now.

I got lost in the rhythm of cooking for myself. I washed a head of romaine lettuce, leaf by leaf, the way I'd seen Mavis do a thousand times before. I scrubbed the cucumber before stripping off its skin and cutting it into circles. Last, but not least, I threw a handful of grape tomatoes into the bowl. A sense of pride which I'd never felt in myself before warmed my entire body. I needed to memorialize this moment so that I would always be able to look back and remember what I'd been through to get here.

Reaching for my phone, some kind of siren sounded. Whirling around toward the stove, I could see it was on fire. In that instance, I froze. What the fuck did I do now? Stop, drop, and roll? Call 911? I shut off the burner in hopes it would stop the fire. That didn't happen, but grease spilled out of the pan onto my wrist when I bumped it with my shaking hands. I wiped my burning arm on my pants.

The fire quickly captured my attention. I could feel the heat radiating from it. My brain shouted at me. I needed to call 911. Where the hell was my phone? I started patting myself down looking for it, but it wasn't in my pants. Shit! Had I left it out in the car?

I raced toward the front door, yanking it open to the sound of more sirens. The neighborhood was lit up with red and white twirling lights. How the hell had the fire department gotten here so quickly? I hadn't even called them yet. Maybe it was Kennedy? As I ran out of the house, I noticed his police SUV wasn't in the driveway. Another neighbor must have called 911.

"Help! Help! My house is on fire!" I screamed when the first fireman climbed out of the red truck. He was a big man, tall and bulky. A long scar stretched from his ear across his cheek.

"What happened?" the man shouted. A tiny smile curved his lips. According to his helmet, he was the captain.

"I was cooking, and my stove caught on fire." Why was this man smiling at me? Shouldn't he be hauling a hose into my kitchen?

"Chasten! Grab the extinguisher!" The captain shouted.

"On it!" the call came back.

I watched in fascination as a younger man opened a panel on the side of the fire truck. He grabbed a fire extinguisher and ran toward my front door.

"Wanna tell me what happened?" The captain was biting his lip in a failed attempt to keep from smiling.

"I was making a hamburger and salad. The next thing I knew, my stove was on fire." My eyes moved back and forth between my front door and the fireman.

"Mmm, hmm," he nodded. The name Graves was on his helmet.

"All set, Captain!" Chasten shouted, closing the front door behind him. He held the extinguisher in one hand. His free hand was raised and fisted like Judd Nelson at the end of *The Breakfast Club.*

Just then, flashing blue and white lights joined the fire department light show. It didn't take a genius to figure out it was Kennedy. I was having that kind of day. The unmarked SUV parked in his driveway and Kennedy stepped out. There was a blue bubble light on the dashboard twirling soundlessly. He wasn't wearing his blues, but instead looked like a pimp. Wife beater, skin-tight black pants, and a huge gold chain. What the hell was going on?

"There was a half empty bottle of cooking oil on the counter near the point of origin. I'm guessing the other half of the oil was in the pan." Chasten slapped a hand down on my shoulder. The name "Coyne" was on his helmet. "Next time you decide to cook, YouTube it." He shrugged and headed toward the firetruck.

"Everything okay here?" Kennedy asked. He was also biting his lip like the dickhead fire captain.

"Yup!" Graves was laughing. "Your boy tried his hand at cooking."

"Oh, yeah? How'd that go?" Kennedy's eyes were on me.

"Crispy would be my guess. Just a little grease fire. Your nosy neighbor, Mrs. Flanagan called it in." The captain laughed out loud. "Later, bro." He headed back toward the fire truck.

"Later, Ozzy." Kennedy watched the fire truck until it was out of sight.

What the fuck was going on here? Why the hell was Kennedy here and why the hell had the fireman called me Kennedy's *boy*? Anger churned in my gut, making my blood boil. I sucked in a lungful of air, ready to launch into a tirade. Meltdown, more like.

"You hungry?" Kennedy asked softly. Without waiting for an answer, he headed toward his front door. "C'mon, let's eat."

My mouth dropped open. I'm sure I looked like a fish out of water gasping for air. In that instant, all the anger passed out of me. I followed behind him like I was his boy.

Kennedy's unit was set up just like my own. The front door opened into the living room, then the dining room. At the end was the kitchen. The only difference between my house and his was that his house looked like a home. A large, overstuffed sectional dominated the living room. There were pictures on the walls above the sofa. Directly across from it was a large television.

"Are you okay? Did you get burned?" Kennedy's questions pulled me out of my head. He was carrying a first aid kit. Just one more thing I had forgotten to buy today.

"My arm." I held it out to him. It was shaking. My entire body was.

"Ouch," Kennedy muttered. He set the kit on the coffee table and started unpacking its contents. "What happened?" His voice was gentle, as were his hands, as he treated my burn.

It was on the tip of my tongue to lie to him, but what was the use of that? I'd made a promise to myself that I'd grow up. "I tried to cook a burger and the pan caught on fire." I sounded pitiful. That was honest enough. I *felt* pitiful.

"Have you ever cooked before?" Kennedy's eyes stayed on my hand. It was as if he knew I couldn't bear to meet his gaze.

"Nah, just stuff in the microwave, popcorn, mac and cheese." I sighed. "It's time for me to grow up, so I figured cooking for myself would be a good place to start."

Kennedy looked up at that. "You are grown up. It doesn't matter if you can't cook. Taking care of yourself is a state of mind."

"You mean it doesn't matter if I burn my house down." Shit, now I was whining.

"Your house didn't burn down. According to Ozzy, it was a grease fire. A little spray from the extinguisher and it was out." He was back to doctoring my arm. I watched, mesmerized as the gauze was wrapped around my wrist.

Snorting, I couldn't help but think I looked like a mummy. "Ozzy?"

"Captain Graves. He's my brother."

That explained a lot. No wonder Kennedy had come home when he had. I looked up at him "Wait. Your last name is Lynch and he's a Graves."

Kennedy's light eyes sharpened on me. He looked as if he were debating something internally. "We're foster brothers. Grew up together." He went back to my wrist, securing the gauze with tape.

Damn… I'd heard of kids growing up in the system, but I'd never met anyone who'd lived through that. I had a feeling I was about to realize that kind of poverty first-hand. My mother's money wasn't going to last forever. I needed to find some way to get back on my feet and fast. I only had enough money to survive for another few months or so.

I was so out of my league here. Twenty-one years old and just barely getting a taste of what *real* life was all about. I'd spent my life being sheltered from the world. I had so much to learn.

"I don't have a lot of time left on my break. Sandwiches will have to do." Kennedy was up and walking back toward the kitchen. "You know how to make a sandwich, kid?"

My eyes rolled of their own free will. "Of course I know how to make a sandwich." It was a lie. I imagined I could figure it out.

Kennedy burst out laughing.

"What?" Damn it, why did he have to be so fucking hot when he laughed?

"I've been a cop for ten years, kid. I know a lie when I hear one." Kennedy reached into the fridge. He came out moments later with his arms filled with sandwich meats, lettuce, and condiments. Lastly, he grabbed a loaf of bread. "Everyone has to start somewhere. Grab some plates." Kennedy pointed to the top of the microwave.

I found myself obeying again. I even managed to keep my mouth shut over Kennedy calling me a kid. I suppose to him I was, not only chronologically, but maturity wise as well. Looking around the house, it was easy to tell Kennedy was a man who had his life together. He had no wife or kids. I reasoned I would have seen them in the various pictures hung all over the house. What he did have was a roof over his head and a job he obviously loved.

Step by step, I watched and then copied Kennedy as he made a ham and swiss on rye. I'd never eaten rye bread before, so this should be an adventure.

"Sit. Eat." Kennedy pointed to the kitchen table.

Again, I obeyed him. I still wasn't sure about the bread until I took my first bite. It was heaven. Christ, how was I my age and had never tried rye bread before? Probably because I was a picky white bread kid. Shit, now Kennedy had me calling myself a kid.

I couldn't help wondering if he was going to join me at the table. Instead of eating his own sandwich, he was making more and shoving them into plastic sandwich bags. He grabbed a reusable grocery bag from a nearby cabinet and started packing the bag.

Damn, there must have been three sandwiches in there. I watched as he added two apples and some small bags of chips. Lastly, he threw in an entire package of Oreo cookies. Damn, how the hell did eat that much and stay in such fabulous shape?

"Here you go." Kennedy set the food-laden bag down in front of me.

"Wait! This is for me?" I couldn't believe my eyes. None of the sandwiches he made were for himself. They'd all been for me.

"Unless I miss my guess, you're not going to burn the house down with these meals. Just make sure they end up in the fridge." Kennedy winked at me.

It was a good thing I was sitting, otherwise I would have fallen down. His words made me go weak in the knees. A new feeling for me. I ducked my head and kept eating, not wanting him to see the effect he had on me. I might be gay, but there was no way of knowing if he was or not. A lot of men were waiting later and later to get married nowadays.

"You want to tell me about what happened to you?" Kennedy took a seat across from me at the table. He swigged from a bottle of water.

The last thing I wanted to do was tell him my sordid story, but since he'd been brave enough to tell me that he'd grown up in foster care, I figured I was brave enough to tell him about the pooch screw that was my life. "My father owns a string of car dealerships. I guess you probably know that." I looked up at Kennedy. He nodded but stayed silent. "He wanted me to follow in his footsteps. I said no. I didn't know what I was going to do, but I knew I didn't want to spend my life selling cars." I shrugged, taking a deep breath. I was waiting for him to roll his eyes or wave me off.

Telling him my story, the way I'd gotten by the first three years of college by the skin of my teeth, before blowing off my final semester of my senior year, I felt lower than I ever had in my life. I'd thrown this information at my father like a drink in his face. I'd wanted to hurt him. Kennedy was a different story. I wanted him to respect me. Maybe. Or like me. Both would have been nice.

"What's next for you?" The question was casual, as if we'd been friends for years instead of minutes.

"I don't know." I met his unreadable gaze. "I need to figure it out fast or…" I didn't want to think about what life would be like for me if I couldn't keep a roof over my head.

"Let's not think about that," Kennedy interrupted, as if he didn't want to hear how my story would end. "A job is the most important thing. Be up early tomorrow morning working on it. Nothing is above you, fast-food, housekeeping, retail. A job is a job. Understood?"

Nodding, I felt my heart sink. If I'd just manned up and finished my damn degree, I wouldn't be reduced to the jobs Kennedy named off. He was right about one thing; beggars couldn't be choosers.

5

Kennedy

Another day. Another scorcher. Or, as they say in New England, scorcha. Either way, it was hotter than Satan's asshole. The blood moon was up to its usual tricks again last night and making matters much worse, there was another fire.

This was the tenth fire and the first one with a fatality. Before last night, the blazes had been set in old mills or other abandoned buildings around the city. This one had been set at a single-family home on the outskirts of town near the Rockport border.

"Christ," I muttered, staring at the remains of the house on Wessex Street. The house was singed on all four sides, with melted vinyl siding dripping toward the ground. All of the windows were blown out, I could see the glass shards sparkling on the lawn. The roof was entirely gone with rays of the early morning sunshine filtering through the remains of the kitchen.

Arson investigation was not part of my training at the police academy. If and when the arsonist was identified, it would be our job to do the background work on the suspect before going out to arrest him or her. It would be the Gloucester Fire Department, in coordination with the Essex County DA's office, who would be in charge of the fire scenes.

"Yeah, Christ is right." Ozzy was standing across from me at what was the front door of the ranch-style house. "Come on, let's get this over with."

Over my career I've walked into many houses my gut warned me not to. This was the strongest feeling of that I'd ever had. There was no one inside with a weapon or holding a hostage, but my body was still thrumming with adrenaline. Taking a deep breath, I followed behind Ozzy.

It was the smell that hit me first. My lungs were filled with the odor of scorched wood mixed with something that smelled like chemicals. I coughed. "What the hell am I breathing?"

"Scotchguard. Possibly household cleaners." Ozzy shrugged. He wasn't having any trouble breathing.

Pushing my own discomfort and feelings of edginess aside, I took a minute to look through the house where an elderly woman had lost her life. The entire living room was soaked and still dripping in spots. Water was puddled near what was left of the sofa. According to Ozzy, that's where the woman's body was found.

I followed him into the kitchen, which was in much worse shape than the living room.

"This is the point of origin," Ozzy said absently.

"How can you tell?" Looking around, everything was burned. How the hell could you figure out where the fire started when everything looked the same?

"Here." Ozzy pointed to a dark spot on the kitchen floor. It looked as if it had burned longer than the rest of the floor around it. "See the melted glass?" His hand went from the twisted glass on the floor, to the window above the sink.

The window was broken, just like the rest of the ones in the house, but I spotted the difference right off. The other windows had blown out, but the shattered glass from the kitchen window was sitting in the sink and on the singed Formica countertop. "The arsonist threw something flammable in through the window."

"Yeah. Molotov cocktail, I'm guessing. This looks like what's left of a bottle of Tito's Vodka." Ozzy knelt down to examine the remains of the glass.

"How can you tell?" I knew damn well Ozzy was right, but I needed to do something to lighten the mood. I could swear I smelled burned human flesh.

Ozzy's dark brow lifted. "Don't be an asshole. How many bottles of Tito's have we knocked back at Bait with Hennessey and Dallas?"

More than I cared to count. "Can we get the hell out of here? This place is creeping me out." Even though Mrs. Genovese had died from smoke inhalation, I could swear I still smelled burnt flesh.

Ozzy shot me a confused look. "You've been at crime scenes much gorier than this, why is this scene upsetting you so much?"

"It's out of my expertise." Finally outside, I sucked in a deep breath of fresh air. That house gave me the creeps in more ways than I had imagined.

"How? You reconstruct crimes all the time. Killers have patterns, so do arsonists. There's something here in this burned out wreck that will connect this fire to the others. I just have to find it."

I knew Ozzy had a point. Unfortunately, I'd also figured out why this burned out shell of a house was making me so uneasy.

"It's your boy, isn't it?" There was no snark in my brother's voice. He'd hit the nail on the head only seconds after I'd figured it out for myself.

"Shit, man, this could have been *him*." Not just the scorched house, but being carried out of it in a body bag.

"I don't mean to be a dick here, but what the hell kind of grown-ass man doesn't know how to kill a grease fire? Hell, the kid's twenty-one years old, why doesn't he know how to make a meal for himself without the GFD having to rescue him and your entire block?" Ozzy didn't just sound angry, there was fear in his voice as well.

The thought that my house could have gone up in flames occurred to me around midnight last night. I had almost been asleep when the image of my neighborhood in flames had me sitting bolt upright in bed, gasping for breath. "I don't know what to say. That kid grew up with all of the advantages of wealth. I'm guessing he didn't have to lift a finger. Not like we did."

Ozzy snorted. "Slave labor! That's what we were to our parents."

I laughed along with him. Growing up in the McCoy household, we all had chores. Each of us did our own laundry and helped cook and clean up from dinner. We were the garbagemen, the landscapers, and the snow removal team. We worked hard, but we all played hard too. "Even when I had blisters on my hands from raking leaves or the beginnings of frostbite from shoveling out the neighborhood, it was still the best time of my life, being part of a real family." I'd said too much. My emotions were about to overtake me.

"Me too, man. Me too." Ozzy gave my shoulder a squeeze. "So, what's new with your boy? He set anything else on fire?" He snorted.

"Gunnar is *not* my boy." I shrugged his arm off me. Ozzy was obviously giving me the business, but I wasn't in the mood for it. My heart still pounded every time I thought about Gunnar and the grease fire.

"Of course he's not." Ozzy crossed his arms over his broad chest. "You just took him home with you like those stray cats you used to rescue. I know you fed him. Did you pet him until he purred too?"

"Fed, yes. Pet, no." Don't get me wrong, I wanted to. Now that Gunnar had dropped the asshole act, he was eminently more petable. If that was even a word.

Ozzy shot me a look that said he didn't quite believe what I was telling him. He should know better. I've got the world's worst poker face. He'd know in a minute if something more than making sandwiches happened between Gunnar and me.

"What's next for him? You said you thought he got thrown out of the house. Does he have a job? Furniture? Food that doesn't need to be cooked?" Ozzy was all business now. He sounded as if he were truly interested in Gunnar's situation. I wasn't a bit surprised. The McCoys raised us with a giving spirit and an attitude of gratitude.

My heart hurt thinking about Gunnar's situation. The go-getter in me had a bit of a different attitude. I stuffed those feelings down deep and tried to be the man my mother raised. "He doesn't have a job, just a few thousand dollars his mother had hidden in a closet. I gave him the any-job-is-a-good-job speech. Don't know if it took. He was supposed to go around town to apply for jobs at McDonald's and Walmart."

"Thousands of dollars hidden in a closet?" Ozzy shook his head. "I'm lucky if I've got twenty bucks left at the end of the week, never mind *thousands*."

"Maybe if you stopped giving money away, you'd have more." I shot my brother a proud grin. Ozzy always gave back to his community. He was truly one of those people who would give you the shirt off his back and the last twenty bucks in his wallet.

Not only was he generous with his money, he also gave freely of his time. My brother volunteered at the local food bank, St. Theresa's Table, coached boys' soccer in the fall, and baseball in the spring. He also volunteered at a local summer camp for kids. He'd bring one of the fire trucks by and let the kids explore it, wear his turnout gear and spray the hose. The kids loved it so much, that Ozzy had gotten Dallas and me to do the same with my police car and one of the ambulances. My brother was a prince among men.

Ozzy waved a dismissive hand at me. "Does Gunnar have any skills?"

"You mean aside from riding my last nerve like it was a bucking bronco?" I wasn't lying. That kid could get my temper to slide sideways faster than anyone I'd ever known, my brothers included.

"Yeah, aside from that." Ozzy looked like he was biting back a smile.

"I don't know. My guess would be no. He was sheltered growing up. I'm not sure he knows how the world works." Not the way I did at his age, anyway.

"Tell you what, if he struck out today at the Golden Arches and Wally World, send him down to the firehouse in the morning."

I was stunned. "What are you saying?"

"There's always something to do at the house. Scrubbing the fire engines, sweeping the floors, cooking, cleaning up, laundry." Ozzy was silent for a minute. "Call it an extension of the McCoy crash course."

Moving in with my foster family had certainly been a crash course in being part of a family and learning how to take care of myself and other people. "It's not a bad idea. He'd learn basic skills under the guise of working for an honest paycheck." The more I thought about it, the more on board I got with the idea. Gunnar would be working for Ozzy instead of being lectured by me. "I'll mention it to him tonight."

Ozzy slapped my back, pulling me into his shoulder for a hug. "Even if he sets the station on fire, we've got people in place who can handle the situation."

Hugging my brother back, I couldn't help wondering what could possibly go wrong.

6

Gunnar

It was another day from hell in a long line of hellish days. I did what I promised Kennedy I would do, and I went job hunting. I dropped applications at McDonalds, Burger King, Wendy's, Subway, two local grocery stores, and Wal-Mart.

The worst part of it had been when the applications asked for references. I had none. I'd worked in my father's dealerships, but I doubted he would do much to help me. I also didn't want him to have any idea I was applying at fast-food restaurants. I used Bryce Hopkinton, after all, he was my landlord. I sent Kennedy a quick text to ask if I could use his name, and when he didn't get back to me, I just decided to use his name anyway. He was the one championing my cause, after all.

The manager at McDonalds had given me the grand tour after he read over my application. He'd raised a silent eyebrow when I told him my name. I knew what he was thinking. Hell, I was thinking the same thing myself. What's a rich-bitch like me doing, applying at the local McDonalds? To be honest, the fryolator scared the pants off me. The good news was that if I got the job, I'd learn how to make a hamburger without burning the place down. He said he'd be in touch after he spoke to my references. I didn't leave empty handed, he'd given me a free meal voucher. I'd used it to buy the biggest meal possible.

It had been the same song and dance at the other places. They'd be in touch. Blah. Blah. *Blah*.

They needed to be in touch *soon*. My mother's closet money-how ironic was *that?*-wouldn't last forever. The one thing I did know was that they hold back one week's salary. So, even if I'd been hired on the spot, I wouldn't have gotten my first paycheck until next Friday.

One extra week without a check meant extra time sleeping on the carpeted floor in my sleeping bag. It was the one splurge I'd made with my mother's money. At least now I wouldn't be snoozing on the bare floor.

After I'd eaten my Double Quarter Pounder with large fries, I got to work checking out what other nearby places were hiring. I avoided Rockport, not wanting to run into any of my parents' friends. Knowing them, they'd only be too happy to run back to my father to say they'd seen me working the fryolator at McDonalds. They might have been rich bitches like my parents, but *everyone* loved a Big Mac from time to time.

The worst part of my day was thinking about Kennedy's reaction to my striking out. Getting a job and being able to support myself was my number one priority now. However, I wasn't any closer to a job today than I had been twenty-four hours ago.

I was off the floor and heading to the fridge when the doorbell rang. Fuck. I didn't need to be a psychic to know it was Kennedy. It was about 2:00 p.m. and his usual shift started at 3:00 p.m. I went to the door and yanked it open. It was Kennedy.

"Did you even use the peephole?" He sounded annoyed with me.

I hadn't. What the hell was a burglar going to steal from me? My sleeping bag? "No. I knew it was you, so I opened the door. It's not like I've got anything worth taking." I ushered Kennedy in, already exhausted from dealing with him.

"No, I guess you don't." Kennedy did a long, slow turn around the empty living room. The anger he'd walked in with seemed to evaporate as he surveyed my nearly empty living room. I'd brought my sleeping bag and pillow downstairs, so I'd be more comfortable as I looked for jobs. "Where's the rest of your things?"

"What things? This is it." I took a seat on the floor. The embarrassment of living in an empty house was too much to bear, especially with the pitying look in Kennedy's blue eyes.

"You had a U-Haul." Kennedy threw his arms wide. "I assumed you had…*things*." His look had turned from pity to shock.

"Yeah, so did I. My mother texted to tell me to come get my stuff. I assumed I'd be able to take my bed and all the other furniture in my room. I was wrong. I got to keep my clothes and my toiletries. And I'm almost out of most of them." I shrugged, hoping it looked careless rather than heartbreaking.

Kennedy's eyes widened at my story. "You don't have a bed to sleep in? Not even an old mattress?"

I shook my head no without meeting his eyes. I'd never been more ashamed in my entire life.

The room was silent. Kennedy hadn't responded to my pitiful head shake. When I chanced a glance up at him, he was texting. It was nice to know I was *less* important than hitting some friend back. My eyes started to roll, but I shut them instead, just in case he was looking at me.

"Okay, I think we'll be able to get you into a bed tonight." Kennedy took a seat on the floor next to me.

"How? You gonna rent me out to one of your friends?" I meant it as a joke, but I could tell by the look on Kennedy's face that it had missed the mark.

"Hardly." Kennedy's look was serious. "Ozzy and Dallas both have some leftover furniture in storage. They're going to check out what they've got. They'll check with our parents too."

My mouth fell open, but no words came out. I think this was the first time in my entire life I'd been speechless. I looked up at him through quickly beating eyelashes. "I don't understand." Not the best line under the circumstances, but I didn't look like a fish gasping for air anymore either.

"We've got some extra things we don't need, and *you* do." Kennedy gave his shoulders a casual shrug. "How did the job search go?"

Just as quickly as my spirits soared, they crashed back to earth. "I put in a bunch of applications. They all said they'd get back to me."

"I was expecting as much. Sorry I didn't get back to you about using me as a reference. I was out with Ozzy this morning at the latest arson scene."

"Arson?" I hadn't heard anything about this. Then again, I'd spent last night cleaning up after my own little fire. Once I'd eaten my salad, I'd gone to bed with music on and had been asleep as soon as my head hit the pillow.

"This is the eleventh fire, but the first where someone died. Ozzy wanted to see if anything caught my eye during a walk through this morning."

"Did something catch your attention?" I liked this, chatting with Kennedy like we were friends.

He shook his head no. "I was having a hard time concentrating because…"

"Because what?" Surely he wasn't upset over my little mishap last night.

"I was worried about you." Kennedy rolled his eyes.

I felt my eyes widen in surprise. I started to tell him I'd been fine but didn't get the chance.

The text tone alerted on Kennedy's phone. "They're here." He was on his feet and heading to the front door. "My brothers constantly give me shit. Don't pay attention to them." With that cryptic comment, he was pulling open the door.

"Step back. Big load coming through." Ozzy was at the front end of a large mattress. A redhead brought up the rear. I assumed that was Dallas.

"Don't stand there gawking, Kennedy. Grab your boy and get the bedrails." The redhead winked at me as he moved past.

A blush bloomed across my cheeks. I ducked my head so Kennedy wouldn't see it. Why was his brother calling me Kennedy's boy? There wasn't time to answer the question. Two total strangers came into the house carrying a box spring.

"You must be Gunnar," the woman said with a bright smile. "I'm Mandy McCoy, Kennedy's mom. I've got more supplies for you in the car, just give me a minute to set this thing down."

"For God's sake, Mandy! It's a hundred and twenty degrees out here. Can you get a move on?" the man at the back of the box spring shouted.

"He's harmless. All bark. No bite." She grinned knowingly at me and started shuffling backward toward the stairs.

"Those were my parents, David and Mandy. In case that all got lost in translation." Kennedy was out the door and jogging down the front steps.

There was a large pick up truck in my driveway. I could see Kennedy wrangling a headboard from the back of it. I raced over to help him. "This is for me?" I still couldn't get over what was happening. Kennedy texted his family and here they all were, bearing gifts. I was stunned. I was so stunned that I couldn't think of another word to use besides stunned.

"You've just been McCoyed, son. As my father would say." Kennedy lifted the bedrails and started back toward the steps.

I'd just been McCoyed. I would never admit it, but I felt all warm inside. Like I was being hugged from all angles. My parents had more money than God, but I could honestly say I'd never seen either of them act like this before. They didn't donate to animal shelters or food pantries. "God helps those who help themselves," my father was fond of saying. I never understood what he meant, since he wasn't a religious man. I got it now. That was his *politically correct* way of saying that he worked hard for *his* money. *You* should work hard for yours.

Dallas and Ozzy bolted past us before we reached the front stairs. "Come on, you two. Gotta be to work in twenty minutes. Move your asses." Ozzy slapped Kennedy's on the way past. I was half afraid I was next. Ozzy was a big man, I bet his hand would leave a mark for weeks.

Fifteen minutes later my new bed was assembled. I was standing in amazement when Mrs. McCoy came back upstairs carrying bags from Target. "Okay, there are sheets and a quilt in this bag." She pointed to a large bag on the floor at her feet. "This one has everything for the bathroom," she called out as she headed into the room. "David's got food and what-not for you downstairs."

"We're off," Dallas announced, before giving Mandy a hug. I couldn't help but notice the way she hugged her foster son, as if he were blood. The hug was repeated with Kennedy, who whispered something to her.

"Try not to burn the neighborhood down, huh?" Kennedy grinned at me before bolting out the door.

"One tiny fire and I'm marked for life." I rolled my eyes.

"One last thing before I go." Ozzy pulled something out of his top pocket and handed it to me. He wore a mysterious grin. "Shift starts at 3:00 p.m. tomorrow. Be there half an hour early so I can give you the lay of the land and explain your duties."

I looked down at what he handed me. It was a business card with his name and cell number. "Wait! You're hiring me to work for you at the firehouse?" In a day filled with surprises, this was the biggest one yet.

"Don't be late, kid. There won't be a second chance." Dropping a wink at his mother, Ozzy was gone.

I turned to Mandy when she started laughing. "I swear that boy is the spitting image of David. If I had a nickel for every time he said that to one of the boys…" She trailed off, turning her attention back to me. "What do you say I help you make the bed?"

I knew what Mandy was doing. She was offering to help in case I didn't know how to make my bed. She hit the nail on the head. I didn't. "Sure." I managed a smile nowhere near bright enough to thank her for what she and her family were doing for me.

"So, Gunnar, tell me about your family." Mandy had the bottom sheet in her hand.

"You got all night?" I started to laugh.

"Tonight, and every night." Mandy gave my hand a squeeze.

I believed her. "My father owns a string of car dealerships…"

7

Kennedy

It was another long shift made worse by full moon madness. Instead of rival gangs beating the shit out of each other, tonight there were two drug-related shootings. Thankfully the victim in the case I'd been assigned to work survived her pimp shooting her in the face. The other working girl hadn't been so lucky. She'd been DOA. I spent the rest of the night working with Detective Mather Welch to compare notes and figure out if our two cases were related.

At the end of our shift we'd been reasonably certain the same pimp had shot both women, but we needed to wait for forensics to come back before making a final determination. In the meantime, detectives from Charlie shift were in charge of going out and finding the pimp, whose street name was Casanova. I'd been so hellbent on catching this motherfucker that I'd nearly volunteered to work a double. Falling asleep for a nanosecond in the Taco Bell drive-thru disabused me of that idea.

All I wanted to do was rinse off in the shower and go to bed. Tomorrow was another day and I needed a good night's sleep for my next shift. I had a plan to run a honeypot sting to round up some of Gloucester's johns.

I noticed my parents were gone when I pulled into my driveway. I had a feeling Gunnar telling his life story to my mother was going to make for a long night for both of them. I wouldn't have been surprised at all to see their car still parked in front of my house.

All the lights in Gunnar's house were on, but so long as there wasn't smoke flowing out a window and the smoke detector wasn't wailing, talking to him could wait until tomorrow.

Nothing felt better than a cool shower on a hot night. Before I'd hopped under the spray, I'd turned the AC down to sub-zero. It was a waste to keep the house that cold when I was at work. It was deliciously chilly when I got out of the shower. I knew sleep was a matter of minutes away, until the doorbell rang.

Pulling on fresh boxers, I hurried down the stairs, still using the towel to dry my dirty blond hair. When I got to the door, I was shocked to see Gunnar through the peephole. "Hey, is everything okay?"

Gunnar's eyes widened in obvious shock. They slowly slid from my chest, down my abs, to my cock, which had woken up under his intense stare.

"My eyes are up here, boy." Part of me wanted to smile so he'd know I was just kidding. The other, horny, part of me wanted to throw him over my shoulder and bring him to bed with me.

Giving his head a quick shake, his emerald eyes met mine. "Uh, sorry. I-I just didn't expect you to answer the door half-naked."

"It's past midnight. The witching hour. What better time to be half-naked?" A tremor zinged through my body. He was still looking at me as if he wanted to take a bite out of me.

"Yeah, sorry about that." He anxiously rubbed the back of his head. "There was something I wanted to talk to you about and I figured after you'd gotten home from work would be a good time. I was wrong. I'll catch you tomorrow." Gunnar turned to leave.

"Freeze." My voice was deadly calm. I saw him shiver in response as he obeyed. Not many people fucked with me when I was in cop mode.

Gunnar turned so he was peering over his shoulder. "Yes, Kennedy."

"In the house now. Don't make me ask you twice." I didn't know what the hell had gotten into me. I was sure the kid was just here to say thank you for everything we'd all done for him tonight.

With a sharp nod, Gunnar walked into the house. I took my time shutting the door. I needed an extra couple of seconds to get my ravenous cock under control. It was hard as stone and snaking up my abdomen. If this kept up, it would be sneaking a peek over the waistband of my boxers any second now.

When I was sure my dick was on the way down, I turned to face him. What I saw had me hard again in an instant. Gunnar on his knees in the center of the living room floor. His head was bowed so that his eyes were on the carpet and his arms were held behind his back. Sweet fucking Jesus. What the *hell* was going on here?

A shiver went through Gunnar. I didn't know if it was because I'd set the air conditioning so low or because he was excited about me seeing him in this light. Had he researched this online or read some BDSM kink somewhere? I had no idea.

Knowing it was the worst possible idea, I walked over to him. "Gunnar?" My voice had gone soft, while my cock was rock solid.

His darkened eyes lifted to meet with mine. I saw hunger and something else I couldn't identify.

I jolted with desire and shock when he set his hands on the back of my naked calves and skimmed their way up past my knees. The boy rose higher on his knees until his face was level with my cock. He licked his lips hungrily before running his tongue over my boxer-clad cock. "I can't thank you enough," Gunnar whispered.

My brain was on overload. His velvet-soft tongue hadn't touched my skin directly, but I still felt the heat of him. The ghost of his tongue lingered on my cock long enough for me to crash back to earth at his words. Wait, he was *thanking* me? "What?" I took a stumbling step backward. My cock deflated faster than an untied balloon.

Gunnar walked forward on his knees to catch up with me. His hands shot out, latching on to my hips. "You did so much for me today. Let me do something for you in return."

Jesus Christ, I *had* heard him right. He wanted to suck my cock to say thank you. "There's a word for what you're proposing. In my line of work, something like this will get you arrested."

"What?" Gunnar's green eyes went glassy. "I'm trying to *thank* you." He scrambled back to his feet, while his hands shot forward to cover his own tenting erection.

"The exchange of goods, services, or cash for sex is called prostitution." My hands were fisted on my hips. I didn't know what pissed me off more, the idea that this kid thought he had to reward my generosity by swallowing my spunk, or the fact that he only wanted to suck me off to say thank you, not because he was into me.

Gunnar stood there with his mouth hanging open. His hands dropped from the font of his pants. There was nothing left for him to hide anymore.

If I didn't say something, this situation was about to go from bad to worse. "Why do you think you have to thank me with sex?" It was the one question revolving in my head.

"How else was I going to thank you?" Gunnar nibbled nervously on his lower lip.

"I don't know, with your *words*, maybe? By not burning the fucking block down? With a card? Anything but by hitting your knees." *For a cop no less*, I couldn't help adding in my head.

One tear streaked down his face. He batted angrily at it. His posture had gone from one of defeat to one of defiance. "Pardon me for not being good enough for your sainted dick." Gunnar turned to go.

It was on the tip of my tongue to stop him, but what was the use? At this point, we'd only end up yelling at each other. With my head still spinning, I watched him go.

Where I'd been ready to go to sleep only twenty minutes ago, I knew after what happened with Gunnar, there would be no sleep for me.

8

Gunnar

Even though the fire station was a five-minute drive from my townhouse, I left an hour before Ozzy asked me to be there. I parked in the municipal lot and tried to get my racing heart under control. Between that and my roiling gut, I didn't know how the hell I was going to make it into the firehouse. All getting to work early did was give me time alone with myself to go over the shit show that had been last night.

What the hell had I been thinking going over to Kennedy's house and offering to whore myself out to him? I'd never been more embarrassed in my entire life.

It had never actually crossed my mind that whoring myself out was what I was actually doing, but whatever. It didn't matter now. I'd gone and killed whatever chance we had to have a relationship of some sort.

Halfway across Kennedy's lawn last night, I'd realized that my first shift at the fire house was twelve hours away. All I could wonder was how the hell was I going to get through that shift with Ozzy knowing that I'd tried to suck his brother's cock to thank him for the job? What the hell was wrong with me?

Maybe Kennedy wouldn't tell him what happened. Yeah, right. Those two were as thick as thieves. Dallas probably knew by now too.

The shakes had hit when I was safely locked in my house. I'd left all the lights on when Mandy and David McCoy left just so I wouldn't feel so alone. Everything I owned, with the exception of my sleeping bag, was thanks to their generosity. How the hell did you say thank you for that?

Apparently, I said thank you with my whorish, cock-loving mouth.

My head sank to the steering wheel. I'd made my bed. Now it was up to me to man-up and sleep in it. With every ounce of strength in my body, I opened the car door and got out. It was hotter than ever this afternoon. I couldn't ever remember a summer that was this fucking hot before. I could well imagine how people without air conditioners must be suffering. Thank Christ my townhouse came with central air.

The parking lot was down the street from the firehouse. When I walked up to it, I could see the large bay doors housing the fire trucks were wide open. There were three fire trucks inside the building, one was a hook and ladder truck. In the fourth and fifth bay were ambulances.

Gloucester had four firehouses spaced out over the nearly forty-two square miles of the city. Each house was responsible for serving one quadrant. If there was an emergency bigger than what one quadrant could handle, a second alarm would be added and other first responders in the city would assist. I'd done a shit ton of reading about the Gloucester Fire Department last night when I couldn't sleep.

My stomach was tossing and turning like a paper boat in a hurricane. I took a deep breath and walked inside. Open-faced lockers lined the wall next to one of the fire trucks. I could see the turnout jackets hung neatly, along with helmets listing the last names of the men and women who donned them.

"Can I help you?" a voice asked from behind me.

Turning, I saw a young man wearing a City of Gloucester EMT uniform. "Yeah, I'm Gunnar Prince. Here for my first day of work. I'm supposed to find Ozzy Graves."

"Oh, you're the new guy." The EMT's dark eyes glowed with a mischievous light. "Come right his way, Newbie. I'm Hal Rossi." He pointed toward the back of the bay and headed in that direction.

If I had never met Kennedy Lynch, I would have thought Hal was the most handsome man on earth. He had jet-black hair and brown eyes with black lines. Tiger eyes, I believe they are called. Hal was much taller than me, six foot, four inches I would guess, with the tightest ass I'd ever seen in my life. A more romantic man would have waxed poetic about how that ass looked like something Michelangelo carved from marble.

"Hey, Cap, your newbie is here," Hal called out as they reached the back of the firehouse. "He's really early, but you know what they say about proper preparation and all that." Hal winked at me as he turned and headed away from Ozzy's door.

From where I was standing, I could see a door with the name GRAVES listed beside it. Screwing up my courage, I poked my head inside the door. "Hey, Ozzy. Here I am."

"Come on in, Gunnar." Ozzy pointed to a chair in front of his desk.

As I moved toward it, I took a minute to look around the room. Ozzy's desk was neat as a pin, no doubt a habit he picked up in the McCoy house. There was a miniature New England Patriots helmet sitting next to his phone and a picture frame facing away from me. Unless I missed my guess, the photo featured his brothers and probably the McCoys.

The wall behind his desk was filled with a huge map of Gloucester. It was one of those old-fashioned ones with fancy scrollwork and what looked like a dragon in the open Atlantic out past Gloucester Harbor. It was gorgeous. Commendations from the mayor and pictures of Ozzy with kids he coached lined the wall to my right. I got the idea that not all his certificates of merit were hanging on this wall. There was probably a drawer in the office stuffed full of others, along with trophies or keys to the city.

When it came to the man himself, Ozzy looked intimidating behind his large mahogany desk. He was leaning forward, making his impressive muscles bunch. He appeared twice his size in that position. I supposed he was doing it on purpose. I relaxed back against my chair and waited for him to speak. His dark hair was cut like he was in the military while his dark eyes twinkled with what looked like laughter. In that moment, I knew Kennedy had told him about what happened between us last night. Christ, I had only been here for five minutes and my battleship was already sunk.

"Wasn't sure if you'd make it today." His tone was matter of fact. The look on his face was unreadable. I wasn't sure if he was serious or yanking my chain.

"Why?" was all I could think to say without giving myself away. If, by some miracle, he didn't know about what happened with Kennedy, I sure as hell didn't want to leave the door open for him to ask about it.

Ozzy gave a casual shrug. "First days are never easy. You've been through a lot. Plus, there is so much unknown about this job. It's not like getting a job at Subway, were you know you're going to be making sandwiches or cutting vegetables all day."

With everything that happened with Kennedy last night, the absolute last thing that had been on my mind was what my job responsibilities would be here at the firehouse. For the first time since I'd left the house, I felt like I was starting to relax. "I understand that you offering me a job here was your way of lending me a helping hand without me feeling like it was a hand out. I'm here to do whatever it is you tell me to do, although I doubt I'm going to be riding a hose during a fire."

Ozzy burst out laughing. "We'll see about that." He slapped one of his large hands against the desk, making the Patriots football helmet jump. "I guess you know how me, Kennedy, Hennessey, and Dallas became brothers?"

I nodded. "He said you were all raised together in the McCoy house." I didn't want to say anything beyond that. What I knew about Kennedy was between the two of us.

"Yeah, that's about the sum of it. The one thing our parents made sure to teach us was to be grateful for everything we had and to do whatever was in our power to help out anyone who was down on their luck."

I knew Ozzy was choosing his words carefully. What he had really wanted to say was that his parents had taught him to help out anyone who was less fortunate than himself. I didn't mind his use of semantics, but on the other hand, growing up the way I did, I could hardly consider myself less fortunate than anyone. "I made some mistakes in my life. Fucking up my opportunity at Boston University is the biggest one of them. I'm hoping today will be a fresh start for me." I meant those words they weren't just useless lip service.

"Just know one thing," Ozzy stood up from his desk. With me sitting and him standing, he looked like a giant. His broad shoulders and larger-than-life personality, only served to make him even bigger. "I'm giving you a chance. What you do with it is up to you. There won't be a second one." His serious face morphed into a brilliant smile. "Now, let's go see my babies."

Following along behind him, I had the opportunity to see how his coworkers and subordinates responded to him. He had a high five or kind word for all of them. It was obvious everyone in the firehouse was a fan of Ozzy Graves.

"There are four firehouses in the city of Gloucester. Mine is number three, that's why all of the fire engines you see here start with the number three. There are sixteen pieces of fire apparatus in Gloucester and they're numbered consecutively. That's why this engine is numbered 313."

"For station three, truck thirteen."

"Exactly. All the equipment is numbered like this so they're easier to keep track of during emergency calls. It also gives the 911 dispatch team a way to speak to the individual fire trucks without needing to know who's on duty during a particular shift." We walked down the line of vehicles. I couldn't help noticing the way Ozzy touched each of them. It was a lover's caress. "Same goes for the ambulances. We have eight that work for the city, so they're numbered in the same way. This is 303 and 304. What each of these babies needs is a nice warm, soapy bath. The buckets and soap are kept in the cleaning locker behind us." Ozzy hooked a thumb in that direction. "The hose you'll use to rinse them off is also back there. May I suggest washing them one at a time, just in case the siren goes off and we have to leave. I guess you're going to end up riding a hose today after all. Any questions?"

I had never washed a car before, let alone a fire engine. I had a million questions, but all of them sounded stupid in my head. I mean, how hard could this be? There was one question that I felt I should ask, especially since Ozzy mentioned the siren. "What happens if you get a call?"

Ozzy's shit-eating grin was back. "Don't tell me you've never seen this on television or in the movies? We all slide down the pole, get into our gear and drive away." He was nibbling his bottom lip to keep from bursting out laughing.

"No, I know *that*. What I meant is what happens to me?" I knew I wasn't going to get to do a ride along or anything cool like that, but I didn't want to be left standing there with my hose in my hand either.

"Worried I'm not going to have enough for you to do, Newbie? All of these floors need to be washed. The stairs leading up to the common area, kitchen, and bedrooms as well. If there are dishes in the sink, wash them. We all know cooking isn't your strong suit, but it's going to be. I'm in charge of all the meal prep in the firehouse on my shift days. In addition to playing the role of Cinderella, you're also going to be my sous chef."

Holy shit. "Is there anything else you need me to do? Shine your shoes? Iron your uniforms?"

The look on Ozzy's face went from amused to serious in a heartbeat. "Listen here, boy. Everyone in this firehouse has a job to do. Shut up. Go with the flow. Do your job. Everything else will take care of itself. Understood?"

Ozzy towered over me. I'd never felt so small in my entire life. I had a feeling that was his exact intent. My heart was pounding in my chest. I'd only been there for ten minutes, and already I was fucking things up. "Understood," I muttered.

"That was the right answer." Ozzy slapped a meaty hand against my shoulder before walking back toward his office. "Oh, and since you mentioned it, Noob, my shoes could use a polish." Ozzy's laughter followed behind him.

"Here, let me help you get started."

When I turned around, Hal Rossi was standing behind me. I'd never been so grateful to see a friendly face in my life. "Thanks, I really appreciate it."

"No, man. I'm the one who has to thank you. Until you got here, I was the newbie." Hal walked me back to the cabinets Ozzy had indicated stored the cleaning supplies. I watched in awe as he pulled out a bright red pail and dumped liquid soap into it.

"But you're an EMT. Shouldn't you be making sure the ambulances are stocked with tongue depressors or something?"

"Like the Cap said, everyone around here has a job. Yeah, we might be firefighters or emergency medics, but we all have to work together to make sure the firehouse runs smoothly. No job is above any of us. You'll even see Ozzy doing dishes from time to time. Whenever one of us sees a gap, we help out. It's the reason the boss didn't give you very many detailed instructions. He knew one of us would step up and do that for him. Now, are you ready to get wet?" Hal dropped me another sexy-as-fuck wink.

I managed to nod. One thing was for certain. Life around Gloucester Firehouse Three was going to be anything but boring.

9

Kennedy

The full moon was at it again. I'd been on duty for three hours and I'd already made five arrests, thanks to a honeypot sting we were running out at the Seaside Motel on Thatcher Road near Good Harbor Beach. Most of the lodgings on that side of town were pretty pricey, but the Seaside had somehow managed to retain its reputation for renting rooms by the hour.

Officer Ella Gutierrez was dressed in a skimpy black halter top with an equally short black skirt that barely covered her assets. What sent the outfit over the top were the red thigh-high come-fuck-me boots. They looked like something out of *Pretty Woman*. She was an absolute knockout and yours for the taking for the bargain basement price of a night in the Graybar Inn, otherwise known as the Gloucester City Jail.

I was in a room next door with Patrolman Anders March and Detective Mather Welch. There were hidden cameras set up in the room Ella was bringing her johns. It was my job to watch the live feed and when the man gave us enough to arrest him. Mather would burst through the door with me hot on his heels to make the arrest. March would be the one to transport the man to the jail.

The night had been going like clockwork until twenty minutes before the end of shift. Ella had one more in-call scheduled, but the man was late. I was in favor of packing up and heading back to the precinct, but Ella and Mather wanted to stick around for the last john.

I didn't know how much more of this room I could take. It smelled of stale cigarette smoke, rancid sweat, and desperation. The john was fifteen minutes late. I was ready to call the op when there was a knock on Ella's door.

We were back in cop-mode instantly. I watched as Ella invited her final client into the room. He was sweating and had a case of the jitters.

I was instantly on high alert. It was a hot night and some men were nervous the first time they paid for ass, but this was different. Anders and Mather could see it too. Both men were tense, and Anders had his right hand on the butt of his gun. "I don't like this," I muttered aloud.

"Take off your top! Let me see those tits," the john demanded. He was sweating more heavily than when he'd walked through the door. His eyes ping-ponged around the room as if he was looking for something.

"Calm down, chico." She offered him an easy smile. "We'll get to that. First we have some business to talk about." There was an uneasy look in Ella's eyes.

"March, go outside to Ella's door, wait for my signal to breach." My eyes never left the screen as the patrolman left the room. "What's our play here?" I wanted to burst into the room and grab the fucker before he could spiral even further out of control.

Mather was standing beside me, to my left. "This is going sideways fast. I say we give her one minute, two at the most to get this guy to agree to pay for sex. If he doesn't, we have to go in there. He's tweaking something fierce. It wouldn't surprise me if he's here to rob her for drug money. He's nearly a foot taller and probably has fifty pounds on her. Ella's tough, but guys on meth have super-human strength."

I agreed with him one hundred percent. Ella's safety was the only thing that mattered now. I was halfway out of my chair when the john reached for her but missed. "Strip, bitch!" He looked around the room again with his crazy eyes. "Where's the money?" His right hand snaked out, grabbing for her upper arm.

Ella was fast, ducking away just in time. He only managed to grab her tank top strap, which ripped under the pressure. "That's it. We're going in there now." I'd seen enough.

"Calm down," Ella was saying. She had backed herself into a corner. The bathroom door was closed behind her and with the way he was advancing toward her, there wasn't enough time for her to open the door and secure herself inside.

"Show me your tits!" The man roared. Reaching behind him, he produced a handgun. With a shaking hand, he pointed at her head.

"Keep him talking, Ella," I said through her earpiece. "Do what you have to do to keep his attention on you. I'll try to sneak in behind him." Fuck, I should have known this bastard had a gun. I should have breached the room sooner when the weapon was still stuck in the man's waistband.

"Okay. Okay." Ella raised her hands in a slow, seductive way. She started teasing her tank top over her stomach. "I'm gonna give you everything you want."

The man's attention was riveted to her. I wasn't going to get a second chance to do this. If he saw me, he was going to turn and shoot. I had no doubt about that. His hands were shaking so badly that I didn't think he would be able to hit me, but I was more worried about Ella. She was only a few feet away from him and if he decided to turn the gun back toward her, there was a greater chance she would be hurt or even killed. "I'm coming in now. Keep his attention on you." Before my eyes left the screen, I saw her black tank top lift over her red lace bra.

I was out of my seat and heading toward the connecting door. "Cover me," I whispered as I started turning the doorknob. This was a shit room in a shit hotel. It didn't have two doors between the connecting rooms, there was only one door with a flimsy slide lock on both sides.

The doorknob creaked in my hand. I froze, my attention back on Mather who was still staring at the screen. He shot me the signal to go ahead. Apparently, the gunman hadn't noticed the squeak.

Pulling the door toward me, I was able to get a look inside the room. Ella had been reduced to teasing her bra straps down each of her arms. I pulled my gun from its holster and took my first step into the room.

"Hurry the fuck up, bitch! This ain't no strip club." The gun was shaking in his hand. The man reached up to wipe the sweat from his brow with his gun hand. The pistol glistened with it.

"Put your hands up, pal." I used my indoor voice, not wanting to scare him too badly. His finger was itchy on the trigger and the last thing I wanted was for the gun to go off in Ella's direction.

He swung toward me, his unfocused eyes were wide. The gun wasn't shaking now. "Fucking pig!" He shouted, his voice ringing loudly against the low ceiling. "Die, you fucker!" He pulled the trigger.

I'd known what was coming and hit the deck just in time. I felt the bullet whistle by my shoulder. It had been a closer call than I'd anticipated.

"You're a fucking cop too, aren't you?" The gunman snarled at Ella. He raised the gun at her. Any vestige of the shakes was gone. The man looked sober as a judge with the exception of his crazy eyes. He pulled the trigger without waiting for Ella to answer.

I had gotten back to my knees when the shot went off. Without hesitation, I fired at him. The back of his head exploded, sending blood and brains splattering onto the bathroom door and wall.

Ella was down. She had a hand clutched to her stomach. Blood was oozing out between her fingers.

"Mather! Get an ambulance here." I heard the motel room door open. "Anders, get me all the clean towels you can find." I hit my knees in front of Ella. Terror and pain warred in her eyes.

"I don't want to die, Kennedy. Please don't let me die." Her dark eyes pleaded with mine.

"You're not going to die, Ella," I reassured her. It was part of our training. If a victim saw a hopeless or scared look in your eyes, they wouldn't fight to survive if they thought the battle was already lost. Blood was pouring out from between her fingers. I hadn't seen the wound yet, but I could already tell this was bad.

"You're going to be okay," I reassured her. Anders' pounding footsteps came toward me.

"These are all the towels I could find." His eyes were wide with the shock of it. Anders March had only been a member of the GPD for six months. This was his first experience with an officer being shot in the line of duty.

"I need to get a look at this, Ella. Anders is going to take your hands away from the gunshot." I nodded at him and he reached for her bloody hands. More blood oozed out. I grabbed one of the towels and pressed it hard against the wound. "Get outside and wait for the ambulance. Make sure they know this is one of our own."

When he was gone, I chanced a look up at Ella. Tears were leaking from her eyes. "Tell my husband I'm sorry. Tell him how much I love him. We had a fight this morning."

The last thing Ella needed now was to be reminded about that. "Look at me, Ella." I waited for her eyes to meet mine. "We're going to get through this together. You'll be back yelling at Javi in no time. I think after this, he might even let you win an argument or two."

Her lips quirked into a quick smile.

I could see her emotions rising to the surface. Detective Gratziella Gutierrez was one tough customer. She was hard as nails, but even the most seasoned cop feared being killed in the line of duty. "It's okay, chica." I gave her my worst Spanish accent. "Everything is going to be okay. I promise I won't let anything happen to you."

"Damn straight, JFK." She raised an eyebrow at me.

I laughed along with her. She'd been calling me JFK since the first shift we worked together. It had taken me two weeks to ask her why she called me that. It turned I was so bossy, she said I was acting cocky like the president. We'd been friends ever since. She kept me grounded and my ego under control. I couldn't lose her.

"Ambulance is pulling in!" Anders shouted from outside the door.

Relief flooded through me. It was going to be okay. Ella was going to be okay. "Listen to me. You hang in there. Fight, Ella. Do you hear me? I'll be there for you every step of the way."

Ella set her blood-stained hands on my own. "Promise," she whispered to me.

I looked up to see Hal Rossi and his partner, Sunny Michaels, run into the room. They were from Ozzy's firehouse. I knew my brother, in one of his engines, was sitting outside too, ready to escort the ambulance to the hospital.

"Jesus, Ella, after all that Taekwondo, I thought you were faster than this." Hal was shaking his head. He set his kit on the floor next to me. "Thanks for the assist, Kennedy. I've got it from here." He rolled his dark eyes. "You believe this? Cop's trying to muscle in on my job."

I knew he was trying to keep her mind off what was going on. I moved out of the way and watched Hal work. I'd known him since he joined the department. Ozzy loved the hell out of this kid. All he did was talk about how lucky they were to have him at the firehouse.

Within minutes, Hal and Sunny had Ella stabilized and ready for transport. I watched as they wheeled her out of the room. Moments later, the twin wails of the fire engine and ambulance sirens sounded.

All I could do at the moment was survey the shitty room. The gunman's blood and brains were drying on the walls. There was a huge puddle of Ella's blood on the floor. Jesus Christ, was it possible for her to survive after losing that much blood?

I knew the Essex County Medical Examiner would be on the way. Same for the crime scene unit. I'd need to get back to the precinct to write up my incident report. Ella was the only thing I could think of at the moment. She'd fought with her husband this morning and might never have the chance to set it right.

I should have called the op when the last john was late. I should have called it when he walked into the motel room. We all had seen there was something obviously wrong with him from the start. We could have burst into the room at the point before he'd had a chance to pull his weapon. For whatever reason, I'd sat on my hands and it almost cost Ella everything. It still could cost her everything.

The one thing I did know, at the moment, was that Ella's blood type was A+. That was one of the things we'd learned about each other when we started working together. I was O-, the universal donor. My first step was going to be to get my ass to the hospital and donate blood.

It was going to take some time for me to get over what happened tonight. A part of me wished I could go home to Gunnar and tell him what I'd seen. There was no way he'd understand. People outside law enforcement rarely did. No. After I donated blood and made sure Ella was safe, I'd pick up a bottle of whiskey on the way home and drown my sorrows alone.

10

Gunnar

I couldn't sleep. The new bed was perfect. It wasn't the problem. My racing mind wouldn't let me rest. It kept bouncing between my first day on the job with Ozzy and Firehouse 3, and Kennedy mobilizing his family to help me out.

We didn't know each other from Adam. Hell, he thought I was a dick the first time we'd met each other. If I were being honest, I was a dick the second time we met too. Yet here I was, lying in a bed with soft sheets that were gifts from his family.

I'd never wanted for anything growing up, but what my parents gave me was out of a sense of keeping up with the neighbors, not out of concern for my comfort. This was different, the kindness of the McCoys was everything.

Half an hour later, I still couldn't sleep. Getting out of bed, I shuffled down the stairs. Maybe I'd feel better after a snack. David McCoy had brought food and a new television the other night. Thanks to him, I wouldn't need to food shop for the next two weeks. A part of me was still struggling with the notion that there were people this good on earth. I was going to do everything in my power to be one of those people.

After wolfing down a banana, I headed outside. The townhouse had a nice little back deck with steps leading down to the backyard. The humidity hit me the minute I walked through the door. I hadn't realized how cold I'd had the A/C set in the house. The warm night air felt good on my clammy skin.

The first thing that caught my attention was the brilliant starfield. I'd never bothered to learn the names of the constellations, but standing here now, I wanted to know what I was looking at. The second thing I noticed was a dark shape on Kennedy's balcony. His deck was only six feet from my own, so I could see him even in the low light. "Can't sleep?" I called over.

Kennedy startled. Maybe he had been sleeping. Or lost in his own private world. "What are you doing out here?" His voice was low. It almost sounded like a growl.

"Uh, this is my house." Shit, I was being a dick again. "I can't sleep," I said in a softer voice.

"Me either," Kennedy admitted. "Is the new bed too soft, Goldilocks?" Even with the joke, the tone of his voice hadn't changed.

I snorted. Ordinarily, I would have fired something back about him being Papa Bear. I didn't. There was something up with Kennedy tonight. Something bad by the sound of it. Instead of being a sarcastic asshole, I tried to think of something a friend or one of his brother's would say to him in this situation. "No, the bed is perfect. My head is still spinning from my shift today."

"You washed fire trucks. How can soapy water keep you up at night?" Kennedy sounded truly confused, but he was still growling.

"It wasn't the bed. It was the gesture. It was given out of kindness. I might have grown up with a rich father, but that doesn't mean he was kind to me." Damn, I was back to sounding pitiful again. Poor little rich boy.

Kennedy stood up from the Adirondack chair he'd been sitting in. He walked to the end of the deck closest to mine. "Did he really kick you out for failing out of school or was there something else?"

There wasn't a lot of light, but I could tell there was something up with him. His eyes looked round and puffy like he'd been crying. If me telling him my coming out sob story would help somehow, I was willing to give it a go. "I always thought my parents knew I was gay. You know how you hear stories about guys that come out and his family asks what took so long? I was hoping it would be like that for me." It wasn't. Not by a long shot.

"Did you tell them during an argument, or during a family meeting when you were calm?" His voice had turned curious.

I knew why he asked the question. I was a sarcastic hothead. Blurting things out was my modus operandi, but not in this case. "There had been so many fights where my father had the upper hand and I just wanted to blurt it out to win, but I didn't want that to be my story."

"That's smart thinking. Once you say the words, you can never take them back." Kennedy's voice was tinged with pride. I can't ever remember someone being proud of me before.

"Right. So, I was home during winter break, and I had a date. A *real* date. He was so cute, and I planned on giving him my virginity. Ramon Cruz was a hottie. He'd been on the basketball team and I never missed a game. He was tall and magnificently built. I wanted to show him off to the world, but my parents needed to know about him first before I took that next step."

Kennedy's shoulders slumped further. I could see he knew how the story was going to turn out.

"I sat them down and just told them I was gay. Neither of them said a word. Their faces were shocked, like they'd never known at all." I could see that moment frozen in my mind's eye.

"That doesn't surprise me. From everything you've told me, it sounds like they were totally into themselves and their lives."

I opened my mouth to shoot something back at him. Kennedy didn't know my parents. How dare he make an assumption like that? Problem was, he was right. He'd also done more for me in the last forty-eight hours than my parents had in my life. "Yeah, that's what I thought too." I shrugged, wanting to be done with this topic, but there was still more to tell.

"How did they respond once they found their words?" Kennedy's voice was gentle.

"My father didn't want to hear any *gay* talk. He stormed out of the room. I tried to explain it to my mother. I told her about Ramon." I could feel my eyes going glassy. The last thing I wanted to do was cry in front of him. "My father stormed back in and told me he'd kick me out on my ass if I went out with a man. I was going to get together with Ramon come hell or high water. I picked a night when my parents were going to their country club for the evening. They were usually out until after midnight."

"I'm guessing they came back early." The earlier pride in Kennedy's voice was now replaced with a bone-deep sadness.

I gave my head a little shake. "My parents caught us and threw us both out." My heart clenched in my chest remembering the crushed look on Ramon's face. "I decided then and there I was done with my father and his manipulative ways."

Nodding, Kennedy moved back toward his chair and sat down hard. It seemed he'd heard enough.

My story wasn't *that* bad. I knew whatever was up with him had nothing to do with me and everything to do with him. I pattered down the stairs in my bare feet. The chilly morning dew soaked my toes. I didn't care. Kennedy had done so much for me, I needed to do something in return for him.

When I reached the top of the stairs, he was sitting in his chair with his head in his hands. There was a faint odor of alcohol on the night breeze. "Tell me about it."

Kennedy gave a bit of a start. He looked at me as if he couldn't believe I was there. His blue eyes were glittering. Unfortunately, they were glittering with sadness. "We were working on a prostitution sting. The last john of the night pulled a gun on the female detective. When I went into the room, he took a shot at me." Kennedy's hands were shaking as he spoke.

I might not know much about police work, aside from what happens on *CSI,* but seeing Kennedy come undone like this, I knew the situation had been hairier than he was describing. "Are you all right?" I couldn't see anything that indicated he'd been hurt, but it was dark out and he was dressed in shorts and a tee.

"I'm fine. The detective playing the role of the hooker was shot. She's in critical condition at Gloucester Mercy." Kennedy gave his head a shake. "The fucker wanted to see her undressed and then he wanted her money. When I came into the room, he fired at me and then turned the gun on her."

I'd seen something about a female member of the Gloucester Police Officer being wounded in the line of duty but hadn't paid any attention to the story. I was so exhausted after the day I'd had at work, all I'd wanted to do was go to bed. "There was a call near the end of my shift. One of the ambulances was sent on a call and Ozzy took one of the fire trucks even though it hadn't been dispatched. My shift was over before they'd come back." Shit, should I have stayed at the station to wait for them?

"Yeah, that was our call. Hal Rossi did one hell of a job with Ella. If she survives this, it will be thanks to him." Kennedy's voice was back to sounding distant again.

Everything made sense now. His strange mood and the off-putting tone in his voice. I had no idea what to do to help Kennedy. I set what I hoped was a reassuring hand on his shoulder.

Kennedy hissed in response. His eyes blazed blue fire, reminding me of the White Walkers on *Game of Thrones.* I backed away from him.

I was sure I'd hurt him, but before I knew what was happening, he was out of his chair and stalking toward me. The way Kennedy moved reminded me of a jungle cat. He was sleek, muscled, and had this look in his eyes that told me I was his prey. A sizable bulge had grown in his shorts. A shiver of apprehension tore through my body when I backed into the deck railing. I was trapped. There was nowhere to go. Straightening my spine, I waited for him to come for me.

He stopped a few inches away. If he moved just a tiny bit forward, his chest would bump mine. I could feel his body heat radiating toward me and could smell the whiskey on his breath. I didn't know him very well, but I got the impression he was letting his dick rule his head in the moment. "That's a good boy," Kennedy muttered under his breath.

Another shiver tore through my body. I'd never been anyone's good boy before, but I wanted to be. Desperately. Not knowing what to say, I looked up at him. His glassy eyes held a note of seriousness and something else I couldn't quite identify. Need, maybe?

Kennedy's hands landed on my hips. His fingers trembled before digging in. His eyes were locked on mine with such an intensity I would swear he could see straight into my soul.

His touch lit a fire in me. I wanted to reach out to him and wrap my hands in the soft fabric of his t-shirt. But I didn't. Kennedy was in charge here and I was going to let his will be done. I would deal with the ramifications of that later.

The grip on my hips eased, as Kennedy slid his hands up my slim torso. He paused, giving each of my nipples a tweak. I couldn't help moaning in response to his touch. My dick was hard and digging into my stomach. I knew he was close enough to feel the heat of me.

Kennedy's hands slid slowly up my neck. If I hadn't been so enamored of what was going on at the moment, I would've been afraid of him. His hands stayed wrapped around my throat for several seconds before they landed on my face. This was absolutely the hottest moment of my life. Every other man I had ever been with couldn't compare to this moment with Kennedy.

The man seemed to be studying me. Looking for what, I didn't know. Maybe he was battling himself. I didn't care. I stood my ground and waited for whatever was going to happen next.

In that instant, his lips were hot on mine. I did reach out, my hands wrapping themselves around his hips only to keep myself upright. If I hadn't reached out to him, I would've ended up in a boneless puddle on the deck.

His right hand slid back down the narrow column of my throat. I could feel his thumb pressing against the pulse point there. My heart was pounding like an out-of-control jackhammer. I knew he felt it, and how much I truly wanted him.

Kennedy pulled his lips away from mine. I had never been more disappointed in my life, until his silky tongue started rubbing against my sealed lips. Everything inside of me wanted me to open up to him, to taste him as he was tasting me, but I didn't do it. I might not ever have the opportunity to kiss Kennedy Lynch again. I was going to make this last as long as I could.

"So sweet," he cooed. Sounding dazed, he licked out over my upper lip, teasing the place it came to a point.

"Christ, Kennedy," I couldn't help moaning his name.

Kennedy took that opportunity to surge into my mouth. Both hands were wrapped around my face again, and I couldn't help feeling a little cherished in that moment. He was such a big man, muscled, and hard. Yet, he was treating me as if I were a porcelain doll.

The moment his tongue met mine, I lost all ability to think. All I could do was cling to Kennedy and trust that he wouldn't let me go. I could feel every muscle tensing his body. He was hard as steel beneath my fingertips, while another impressive and hard part of him nudged against my thigh. It was in the back of my mind to reach out for it and give him a little pleasure on what had to be a god-awful night for him, but I reigned in my own desire and let him set the pace.

Without warning, Kennedy pulled back from me. His eyes were filled with passion, but his body language told me something had thrown a bucket of cold water on him. Maybe his heart, but most likely his head. "Good night, boy." With those words, Kennedy turned from me and went back into the house. I heard the sliding glass door lock into place and after a few seconds, the privacy blinds settled back into place.

My heart was still racing, and my dick was still hard as stone. I gave one last look to Kennedy's closed door and headed back to my house. I had a feeling I wasn't going to sleep for a while yet.

11

Kennedy

I woke up to a text jingle from my captain, telling me Ella was still in ICU, but had been upgraded from critical to critical, but stable. Which meant she hadn't gotten any worse overnight. The surgery to remove the bullet had been successful, but she'd lost a lot of blood.

Thanks to hospital regulations, I had only been able to donate one pint. I would've given so much more if I had been able to. Ella meant the world to me and I would do anything to make sure she came through this healthy.

Her husband, Javier, had come to see me while I was in the donation room. He, of course, had asked if his wife had said anything before she'd been taken away by the ambulance. I wasn't going to tell him what she had said to me about their fight, but since he had asked me to my face, I felt like I didn't have a choice.

Javi had been in tears by the end of my story. Not only had I told him what Ella said, I also gave him a quick rundown of exactly what had happened in that shitty motel room last night. I had planned to work on my incident report while the hospital vampires drained me, but in the end, I was glad I'd had a chance to deliver Ella's message.

My brother, Ozzy, had called when I was in the shower. He was on his way to visit Ella and asked if I would meet him at the hospital. I could only draw one conclusion. He wanted to talk to me about Gunnar. Fuck me gently with a jackhammer.

Of course, the boy wonder had been on my mind since I'd kissed him last night. I still didn't know what had gotten into me. What the hell had I been thinking kissing him like that? Not that it hadn't been the most explosive kiss of my entire life. Christ, I'd only been seconds away from taking him right there on the back deck. Gunnar had been just as hard and ready to go as I was.

The only thing that stopped me from fucking my neighbor like a caveman was a flashback to what happened in that motel room. I could see Ella down on the filthy floor with her blood pouring out over her hands. I'd backed away from Gunnar like I'd been burned.

I suppose, in a way I had been. In my thirty years, no one had ever kissed me like Gunnar Prince. He kissed me like I was his oxygen and he'd die without my lips pressed to his. Making my cock even harder was the fact that he'd been so sweetly submissive. Thinking about it now was making my dick hard all over again. I was thankful, in the light of day, that I'd walked away when I had.

Catching sight of the hospital was enough to quell my growing hard-on. Knowing my brother would be waiting for me in the lobby served to throw a second bucket of ice water on my hormones. I could only imagine Ozzy had bad news for me and that, coupled with Ella being in the fight for her life, thankfully took my mind off my dick and Gunnar, to some degree.

Ozzy was waiting for me in the large, open atrium of the hospital lobby. "Hey, man." I didn't give him a chance to return my greeting but pulled him into a hug.

"Are you okay?" Ozzy mumbled against my shoulder, before pushing me back to take a peek at my face. He was looking me over like my mother would have, had she been here.

I knew in that moment I was screwed.

"What the hell happened to you? Jesus, you look like something out of *The Walking Dead*. Shit, half of those zombies look *better* than you. Come with me." Without giving me a chance to answer or protest, Ozzy was dragging me toward the elevator bank. I knew we were headed toward the cafeteria. Having known my brother for nearly twenty years now, I knew he listened best with a full stomach. It was a McCoy family tradition to talk things out over cookies and cocoa. Later it had been lattes and then cocktails. With it being morning, I'd settle for some juice and chocolate pudding.

My brother was silent as we rode the elevator down a level to where the cafeteria and the respiratory therapy team was housed. There were other people in the car with us, but he wouldn't have said another word even if we'd been alone. It was just how Ozzy worked.

The cafeteria was nearly empty. There was an older couple with cups of coffee in front of them, looking as if they were preparing for the absolute worst. I knew the feeling well. That feeling and I had become acquainted during my childhood when one of my mother's boyfriends would lose his temper and it continued on through today with my current situation. My partner was clinging to life in the ICU and my brother was about to drop a bombshell. Thankfully, there was pudding.

I grabbed a table as far away from the other couple as possible. From where I was sitting, I could see Ozzy chatting with a man in a white lab coat. He tried to keep it on the downlow, but I saw him take the other man's phone. Obviously, they were exchanging numbers. Go, Ozzy.

"Did you see that? Damn, that man was *fine*." Ozzy was all smiles as he sat down at the table. He'd gotten a giant coffee and two large muffins. The one he tore into was blueberry.

"Yeah, I saw him." I couldn't have been less interested in this conversation. I know my voice conveyed that loud and clear.

Ozzy shot me a frown. His scar twisted with it. "Look I get that your friend is in the hospital, but word in the ICU is that she's going to pull through this and with a little PT after she's healed, Ella will back to work in no time."

"Nice of you to save that crucial information until now. Jesus, Ozzy! I've been upset enough over what happened to Ella. Why the hell would you drag out my worry?" I'd always had trouble with anxiety. Just another one of the many gifts from my mother's string of men. Anxiety. Panic. Cigarette burns. Near molestation. Those men had saddled me with so much shit over those formative years. It was a wonder I wasn't a broken-down drunk living under a bridge. The McCoys had truly saved me in every way possible.

"Hey, I'm sorry." The shit-eating grin on his face morphed instantly into concern. "I thought you knew about Ella."

"Yeah, well, I *didn't*. Not only did I have to worry about her, I'm also on edge about what you need to tell me. I know this has something to do with Gunnar. Just say it and get it over with. Like ripping off a Band-Aid. If you have to fire him, just tell me." I sat up straighter, bracing myself for whatever bad news Ozzy had for me.

His serious face broke into grin. He barked out a quick laugh before he managed to get himself back under control. "I do want to talk to you about Gunnar, but *not* because I want to give him the boot. He was phenomenal yesterday."

"He was?" I cleared my throat loudly. "Of course he was." I sounded more confident now.

Ozzy shot me a yeah-right look. "I practically threw him to the wolves. Told him he would only get one chance and then sent him off to wash the engines with no instructions."

I snorted. I'd heard from other recruits and rookies what a task master Ozzy was. There was no way in hell I would ever work for him. We'd be at each other's throats within the first ten minutes. "That's a little cruel, don't you think?"

Ozzy devoured half of his second muffin in one huge bite. "Nope! I knew if the kid was humble and admitted what he didn't know, people would help him. Lo and behold, someone did help him." Ozzy took another bite. "And, if I were you, I'd stake my claim on that boy while the staking is good."

"What the hell are you talking about?" Staking my claim? My brother had definitely gone off the deep end.

"I've got two words for you, little brother." Ozzy's left eyebrow lifted toward his hairline. "Hal Rossi."

"I just saw him yesterday." He'd been one of the EMTs who'd saved Ella.

Ozzy's left brow shot sky high. "That's *all* you have to say about Hal? Christ, if you don't think that man is the handsomest fucker on earth, I'll eat my napkin."

Of course I thought Hal was handsome. With his dark hair and his easygoing manner, the man was an absolute ten. He reminded me of a young Robert DeNiro, minus the large birthmark on his cheek. I did remember joking with Ozzy about wanting to find out where Hal's birthmark was. "He's cute."

"*Cute?*" Ozzy waved a dismissive hand at me. "You've lost your fool mind and you're about to lose your boy too. He and Hal spent the entire day working together yesterday."

That gave me pause. Momentarily. "Until you hired Gunnar, Hal was your last newbie. All the things you'd saddled Hal with, in addition to his actual duties now went to Gunnar. He's the kind of guy who would appreciate that and do what he could to help out the new newbie." I hoped.

"Jesus, Pollyanna. *No one* is that altruistic. People do things for other people because of what's in it for them. Hal helped Gunnar because he's interested in him." Ozzy took a sip from his coffee cup. His eyes never left mine.

Anger was roiling in my gut. "Why is this so important to you? Jesus, Christ, Ozzy! If you're that bored, go out and get yourself a twink for the night."

"Is that what you think this about? Me being bored." He stood up from the table gathering the muffin wrappers and his cup of coffee. "When was the last time you had a meaningful connection with another human being, Kennedy? Not a one-night stand or small talk with the grocery store checkout person? Here I am, trying to help you out and you're being a dick. There's something between you and this kid and if you want to deny that, it's on you. Later." With those words, Ozzy was gone.

I sighed as I watched him walk away from me. Was I being a dick? Yes. Was there something between me and Gunnar? Also, yes. The problem was that I had no idea what it was. One night I'm pushing him away from me and the next night, I'm the one pulling him close.

Maybe there was something between me and the kid. All I knew at the moment was that I was more confused than I'd ever been over a man.

12

Gunnar

An early morning text from Ozzy had me up at the ass-crack of dawn on my first day off in nearly a week. My boss wanted to see me at the station within the hour.

I was in a near-panic. I'd showered as quickly as I could and practically flew down to the firehouse. Thank goodness I hadn't been pulled over by the Gloucester P.D. I may have an unpaid parking ticket or three which would have complicated matters even further.

After I parked the car, I took a few deep breaths to get myself back under control. The last thing I wanted to do was race into the station out of breath and asking where the fire was. When I was as calm as I was going to get under the circumstances, I got out of the Dodge and headed toward my doom.

I'd thought my first week on the job had been a good one. I did everything that had been asked of me without lip or complaint. There had been *so* much to complain about. Cleaning the engines and helping Hal stock the ambulance was fine, but having to keep the shitters clean? Motherfucking eww. It had been on the tip of my tongue to ask the firefighters if they were shitting big on purpose this week. You know, saving it up for work. There was a constant stream of skid marks in the bowls. Somehow, I'd managed to keep my mouth shut.

The only way I'd gotten through it was by singing the score to *Wicked* while I scrubbed the skids away. After day two of that, half the house had told me I was a dead man if they had to listen to *Defying Gravity* one more time. I stopped short of telling them they wouldn't have to listen to my shitty *Wicked* if they stopped taking wicked shits.

Aside from my penchant for showtunes, I couldn't think of any other reason Ozzy would want to can me. I supposed I was about to find out.

The bay doors of the firehouse were wide open. All three of the engines were gleaming in the morning sunshine. I walked past the lockers filled with turnout gear stowed neatly on pegs. I couldn't help but wonder if this would be the last time I'd walk into this building as part of the team. Part of the family.

My stomach was twisted in knots and my heart hammered in my throat as I approached Ozzy's door. When I worked up the courage to peek inside, his office was empty. Fuck. Fuck. And fuck again. Now what?

"Hey, Noob! Up here!" a familiar and very jocular voice shouted. "Move your ass! These ribs ain't gonna cook themselves."

When I looked up to the second floor, Ozzy was standing at the railing grinning down at me. Ribs? What the hell was he talking about?

I hauled ass up the stairs. My mouth dropped open when I saw Ozzy. He was wearing a black apron with *Kiss the Cook* printed on it in red letters. On the counter near the stove were several racks of ribs and what looked like the entire spice aisle from the grocery store. "What is all of this?"

"It's Sunday!" Ozzy announced cheerfully.

"On Sundays, we cook!" Hal Rossi said from behind me.

"We do?" I was still feeling confused as fuck, but at least my doom didn't seem as imminent as it had moments ago.

"Yes, we do." Ozzy was all smiles. "Now get over here and make the dry rub."

"Dry rub? What the hell is that? Sounds like a bargain basement hand job from a sleazy massage parlor."

Hal snorted behind me, but Ozzy looked like I'd just insulted his mother. "What's a dry rub? You really are a caveman. If you can read, you can cook. At least that's what my mother always told me. Get over here and read the recipe. Do you have any idea how to use measuring cups or spoons?"

I had no fucking idea what Ozzy was talking about. My heart was still pounding. All that mattered was that I wasn't getting fired. At least I thought I wasn't. Maybe this was some kind of last meal like death row inmates got before they rode the lightning.

Regardless of my measuring spoon knowledge, I did what Ozzy asked. There was a stained paper recipe sitting on the counter alongside the flock of spices. Cumin. Paprika. Garlic powder. Coriander. Cayenne. I didn't know most of the words, but thankfully the jars were labeled.

"Let me guess, you've never cooked with a recipe before." Ozzy crossed his arms over his broad chest.

"I'm more of a read the instructions on the box type." I felt my lips curl into a smile. The boulder sitting on my chest loosened.

"Uh, huh. Well, I'll walk through it with you the first time. Next time, you're on your own."

"Next time? You mean you're not feeding me a last supper before cutting me loose?" My mouth hung open like a fish out of water.

"Cutting you loose? What the hell are you talking about, kid?" Ozzy's dark eyes seemed to be assessing me. Reading me. "You had a great first week. Everyone thought you'd be a stuck-up prick, but they all love working with you. Some of the guys have stopped by my office to tell me personally."

I was stunned. My parents constantly told me how selfish I was growing up. I hadn't had a lot of friends. Most kids my age were more interested in my parents' money than they'd been in me. Here I was, though, popular and well-liked at my job. "I don't know what to say to that." I could feel my emotions rising.

Ozzy set a hand on my shoulder. "I think you've found a *home* here." His warm hand gave my shoulder a squeeze and then was gone.

I had a feeling Mandy McCoy had said that exact sentence throughout Ozzy's childhood. It gave me the warm fuzzies. I didn't think I was a warm fuzzy kind of guy until I met these people.

Slowly but surely, Ozzy and I worked together to make the dry rub. I got to be the one to mix all the spices together. Seeing all the different colored powers get dumped into the bowl, I wondered more than once how all of these things could come together into something that would taste good. Now that they were all combined, I was in heaven. It was hard to resist the temptation of sticking my finger in the bowl for a taste.

"Now, we rub the meat." Ozzy's dark eyes glowed.

"Excuse you?" a familiar voice said from behind us. I knew in an instant it was Kennedy.

Ozzy started to laugh. He handed me transparent gloves. "Don't let my brother fool you. He's a meat rubbing champion! Gave himself Carpal Tunnel Syndrome when we were teenagers."

"Jesus Christ, Oz!" Kennedy blushed furiously.

"Don't be such a puritan. We've all been hand-to-gland combat champions at one time or another." Ozzy donned a pair of gloves himself and scooped up a small handful of the dry rub.

I watched him rub it on the first rack of ribs, but my head was somewhere else. All I could think about was Kennedy touching himself. How did he do it? Was it a race to the finish line? Did he take his time with long easy strokes? Or was it something in the middle, starting off slow and building at the end?

"Kid?" Ozzy nudged my shoulder, breaking the spell.

Fuck, I could feel the heat in my face and knew I was lobster-red, like Kennedy. "Yeah, I got it."

"You ever think another man would have to teach you how to rub your meat?" Hal Rossi asked. He was sitting at the main dining table across from Kennedy.

"I never expected my education to be so thorough." That was true. Ozzy was rubbing on those ribs like he was about to propose.

"You're missing the point of the dry rub." Ozzy's tone reminded me of the way you'd speak to a toddler.

"Enlighten us, Master Bator." Kennedy executed a perfect mock bow.

"No ribs for you!" Ozzy pointed at his brother, with spices sprinkling from his gloved hand. He turned back to me with a some-people look on his face. "The ribs are going in the oven to roast low and slow. During that time, the rub will marry itself into the meat, flavoring it."

"I'm confused." I heard Kennedy snort behind me. "Why do we rub the meat only to slather it in barbeque sauce?"

"Since Kennedy seems to have all the answers, he can enlighten you." Ozzy crossed his arms over his chest.

"It builds the *layers* of flavor." Kennedy rolled his eyes, acting as if he'd been schooled repeatedly on this very topic.

"Very good." The sass was obvious is Ozzy's voice.

"The two of you have such a great relationship." I looked back and forth between them. Truth be told, I was a little jealous of the obvious love between the brothers. Being an only child had its plusses and minuses. The biggest minus was not having anyone with my same shared experiences. "Have you two always been this close?"

The grin faded from Ozzy's lips. I couldn't help noticing how the look on Kennedy's face turned equally serious. Oh shit, I must have really put my foot in it.

"I was terrified of him," Kennedy said softly.

"I hated him on sight." The same sad tone filled Ozzy's voice.

Oh, fuck. What had I done? My mouth fell open. For the first time in my life, I was at a literal loss for words.

"Close your mouth, kid. You'll let in flies." Ozzy went back to rubbing the ribs with the spice blend. "Here's a newsflash for you, the *Brady Bunch* isn't real life. You don't get sent to a new home with total strangers and everything is hunky-dory in thirty minutes. It sure as hell never worked that way for me and I was in four foster homes before I landed with the McCoys."

I felt my mouth start to drop open again. Until I had to bunk in with my friends over the last few months, I'd only had one home. In a very distant way, I had some idea of what the brothers had gone through bouncing from house to house after I'd been kicked out of my own, but that happened when I was twenty-one years old and was of my own doing. Ozzy and Kennedy had been little when they were put into the system.

"Ozzy, Dallas, and Hennessey, of course, already lived in the house. I was the new kid on the block. The interloper, so to speak." Kennedy stood up and started pacing around the dining area. "My mother had just been murdered by her boyfriend and right after they wheeled her body out on the gurney, I was being told to pack my things and was hustled out the door. Two hours later, I was being dropped on Mandy and David's doorstep."

My left knee buckled, threatening to send me crashing to the floor. Thankfully, Ozzy grabbed my right arm and kept me on my feet.

"Pull it together," he whispered in a voice low enough that I was the only one who could hear him.

Shit. What the hell did you say to that kind of story? "I'm so sorry, Kennedy. I had no idea."

Kennedy gave me a half-hearted shrug. "How could you have known? Anyway, when I was introduced to the McCoys it had already been the worst day of my life. I sure as hell wasn't in the mood to make friends with total strangers. Plus, Ozzy had that scar and he was growling at me."

"For fuck's sake, Kennedy! I've told you a million times, I wasn't growling at you."

"He was growling," Kennedy affirmed. "Ozzy wanted me to know he was the baddest bitch on the block." Both men burst out laughing.

"I was supposed to sleep in Hennessey's room. Mandy and David always put the new kid in with him. I had no idea that Ozzy was so attached to the room. If I had known, I would have slept in the room with Dallas instead." Kennedy waved a dismissive hand toward Ozzy. "I still have no idea why you liked sharing a room with Hen. He snored like a freight train even at the age of twelve."

Ozzy shrugged. "It was the first real room I had that was safe. I'd gone from house to house and none of them felt like a home until David and Mandy."

Kennedy sat down hard. "I had no idea. Shit, man, why didn't you tell me?"

"Oh, you know how Mandy wanted us to be nice to the new kid. Make him feel welcome. Don't make waves."

"You know, I heard that speech so many times while we lived there. It never crossed my mind that you all made sacrifices for me." Kennedy looked humbled by his realization.

Ozzy stepped away from the ribs, pulling his gloves off. He headed toward Kennedy, stopping a few feet in front of him. "I was really only mad about that bed for the first night."

"What changed your mind?" A grin played around Kennedy's lips.

"You mean aside from the fact that Dallas doesn't snore?" Ozzy started to laugh. He pulled Kennedy into his arms for a hug. "Love you, little brother."

"Right back at you." Kennedy mumbled.

I was still dumbstruck by what I was hearing. Looking at Hal, I could see he was feeling the same way. Part of me wanted to cry for ten-year-old Kennedy and what he'd gone through. The other part wanted to hug him until my arms fell off.

It just seemed so unfair, me growing up in the lap of luxury and Kennedy not having the most basic of comforts, a home, a mother, safety. I straightened my spine and went back to work preparing the food. There would be time to cry for that little boy later.

13

My conversation with Ozzy and Gunnar left me feeling shaken. It wasn't very often I spoke about my childhood or the night I landed on the McCoy's doorstep. I'd been a terrified little boy left in the care of complete strangers. Having to unpack that baggage in front of Gunnar, who'd never wanted for anything, was more emotional than I'd expected.

Ordinarily, I would blow off questions about my time in foster care. If I had a nickel for every time I refused to talk about it, I would be the one living in August Prince's mansion instead of my townhouse.

Of course, it wasn't any more Gunnar's fault for the way he grew up than it was mine. But it made me feel less than, which twenty years later should have been ridiculous, but somehow wasn't.

After my brother finished hugging me, he'd gone back to Gunnar and put the meat in the oven. That's not where his day in the kitchen ended. Ozzy handed him a potato peeler, which the kid had looked at like he wasn't sure what the hell it was. That look was nothing compared to the utter shock on his face when Ozzy set a ten-pound bag of potatoes in front of him. I wish I'd had my phone out for that.

After Gunnar peeled the potatoes, it was time to shred the cabbage and carrots for the coleslaw. He'd even made the dressing rather than using a bottled one. Next was the jalapeno corn bread, which was an adventure in itself when Gunnar touched his face after he'd cut the peppers.

Last was the barbeque sauce. I knew instantly when Gunnar was gathering the ingredients that it was our mother's secret recipe. The *secret* was that we all knew it had come from an old copy of the Woman's Home Companion Cookbook.

As the morning rolled on and Ozzy taught Gunnar to cook, I used that time to study him. He never backed away from a challenge or acted like any of this was beneath him. More importantly, he was giving as good as he got from Ozzy. My brother could be an intimidating S.O.B., something I learned well the night we met, but underneath that battle-worn shell was a heart of gold.

While they continued to cook and bullshit each other, I grabbed plates and started to set the table. When I was finished, Gunnar studied each place setting before heading off to the can. I assumed he was memorizing the set up for next time.

I saw a different side of Gunnar that morning. I grudgingly came to admit that it wasn't his fault that he'd never learned to make a meal, set a table, or wash dishes. The problem with getting to know the new and improved Gunnar was that he made me want to fuck him that much more.

"Okay, everyone! Chow time!" Ozzy called out to the entire firehouse.

Ozzy's booming voice startled me out of my own thoughts. Before I knew what was happening, the other firefighters and EMTs filled the room, taking seats at the long table. The head of the table and the seat next to me were left open. I knew Ozzy sat at the front, which meant Gunnar would be next to me. It was the last thing I needed with my dick half hard in my pants.

When everyone was seated, Ozzy and Gunnar started bringing the food to the table. We'd always eaten family-style at home. My brother had continued that tradition at the firehouse which was his second home.

"I know everyone is starving. I've been listening to Kennedy's stomach grumble for the last hour." The table erupted in laughter. "But, before we eat, I want you all to give it up for Gunnar Prince, who I met when he set his house on fire cooking a hamburger." Ozzy snickered and elbowed Gunnar, who was laughing too. "He did a hell of a job in his first week here and only managed to cut himself once with the potato peeler."

"Gunnar!" The table chorused. Polished boots stomped the floor.

I couldn't help noticing the way Hal Rossi looked at him. Ozzy had a point when he said the young EMT had the hots for my boy. Not my *boy*. My *neighbor*. Yeah, my neighbor. And if that were truly the case, my dick wouldn't be digging into my stomach.

"Thanks everyone for making me feel like I'm part of your family," Gunnar's eyes had gone glassy as he looked around the table.

"Let's eat!" Ozzy announced, sitting down at the table. It was obvious he was giving the kid the opportunity to regain his composure. I knew him, chances were that he'd had a longer speech planned out.

The cornbread was in front of me. I grabbed a piece and set one on Gunnar's plate before passing it to Ozzy who shot me a knowing look.

Ten minutes later, everyone was eating and talking with the people sitting close to them. I'd been to so many of these Sunday dinners that it felt old hat to me, but I knew how exciting this must be for Gunnar. Not only had he been invited here on his day off, but he'd gotten to cook with the captain, which was a bigger honor than he knew. Ozzy didn't let many people into his kitchen.

"Damn, this is the best thing I've put in my mouth since Kennedy…" Gunnar's mouth slammed shut with an audible click of his teeth.

"Since Kennedy, *what?*" Hal leaned toward Gunnar, his eyelashes fluttering.

"Since I dropped off lunch from China Jade yesterday."
Christ, that was close. I knew exactly what Gunnar had been
about to say. The ribs were the best thing he'd tasted since I'd
forced my tongue down his throat.

"Yeah, the beef and broccoli plate was amazing. The Chinese
place we used to go to in Rockport sucked, but this food was
off the hook. Crispy Rangoon and tender…meat." Gunnar
wore a miserable look on his face.

"There's nothing better than tender and juicy meat in your
mouth." Hal seductively licked barbeque sauce off his finger.

Motherfucker. Christ, if this kept up, the EMT was going to be
fucking my boy in no time flat.

"When do I get to go on a ride along?" Gunnar asked after
Chasten handed him the platter of ribs for a second helping.

Ozzy's face morphed into a devious grin. I knew exactly what
that smile meant: be careful what you wish for. "You want to
go on a ride along, Noob? I think we can arrange that."

Hal Rossi started to snicker. Looking around the table, the
others were hiding smiles behind their hands.

"Okay, what does that mean?" Gunnar's head swung around like it was on a swivel. His dizzy gaze finally landed on me. "Kennedy?"

"I don't know what that means." I shot Ozzy a what-the-fuck look, but all he did was continue to laugh. "When we do ride alongs at the GPD we get assigned traffic stops or meter patrol. Simple things that don't usually put the civilian in harm's way." It didn't always work out that way, but that was our aim.

"You're not a member of the Gloucester Police Department, you belong to Firehouse Three. Now, either you mean what you said about coming with us on a call or you didn't." Ozzy grabbed the meat platter from me. I managed to grab another rib with my fork as he pulled it away.

Gunnar sat up straighter. "I meant what I said." The earlier insecurity in him was gone.

I was going to have a conversation with my brother about what this ride along included. Since Gunnar wasn't licensed by the Commonwealth of Massachusetts, he couldn't handle the equipment or drive the engines. The last thing I'd accuse my brother of was hazing, but at the same time, I didn't want anything to come between Gunnar and the new family he was building. Ozzy should know that better than anyone.

"Hal, tell him about your first ride along." Ozzy was back to wearing that shit-eating grin.

At least if he was asking Hal to tell the story, it couldn't be all that bad. From everything I knew about him, he got along well with everyone at the firehouse and had a close relationship with Ozzy. According to my brother, he wouldn't be surprised if Hal was promoted to captain within the next five years.

"It was wild, that was for sure." Hal burst out laughing with the others.

"Define *wild*." I wasn't in the mood to mince words.

Hal opened his mouth to answer when his stomach gurgled loudly. His face twisted into a grimace and he slapped his hand over his mouth. It didn't help. His cheeks bulged like a chipmunk and before he could get out of his seat, Hal started to spray puree through his fingers.

Looking around the table I could see a few other firefighters looking a bit green. I didn't think it was from seeing Hal lose his lunch. Firefighters and EMTs were used to this kind of thing. Someone gagged and sprinted away from the table.

What the hell was going on here. One by one, members of Firehouse Three sprinted from the table.

Holy shit, had Gunnar given the entire firehouse food poisoning?

14

Gunnar

It didn't stop with Hal losing his lunch. Chasten was next and then Ozzy. Several of the other firefighters wandered away from the table with sour looks on their faces. My mother had always been a sympathetic barfer. If she so much as heard someone gag or smelled regurgitated chum, she would blow chunks too.

This was a disaster. I'd never seen anything like this before. I watched as one brother after another got sick. Some scrambled to the restroom downstairs, while others ran to the toilets in the bunkhouse. I'd even seen a few of the guys run into the ladies' room.

The only two people left standing at the end were me and Kennedy. He was wearing a look on his face that was somewhere between shock and awe. "Um, Kennedy, what do I do now?" I had no idea what was going on, much less what to do next. The entire firehouse, with the exception of me, was puking their guts out. If the sounds coming from the bunkhouse were any indication, it seemed that a new symptom had entered the playing field. I could hear the men throwing *and* going, as the saying went.

"If I were you, I'd run," Kennedy said simply, getting out of his seat. His gaze was directed at his feet. Ozzy had left a slurry trail as he'd run for the closest toilet.

"Run? I don't understand." I was more confused than ever, unless Kennedy meant that he wanted me to get out, so I didn't catch this bug too. The rough tone in his voice indicated otherwise.

"Kid, you just poisoned the entire firehouse. Hell, I'm not even sure what the protocol is here. If that alarm bell goes off right now, no one is available to go to the call." Kennedy pivoted around in a neat circle. He looked overwhelmed by the situation. "I need to call the fire chief and see what can be done."

"Now hold on just one minute!" I shouted at Kennedy's retreating figure. "I didn't poison anyone." At least I didn't *think* I did. Terror like I'd never known in my life gripped me. What if Kennedy was right? What if I did this? An hour ago, Ozzy was calling me a member of the family and now he was bowing to the porcelain god. What the hell had I done?

"Start cleaning this up. Put on gloves. Throw all the food away. After that, mop up the puke." Kennedy grimaced, before giving his head a shake. "Fill a bucket with disinfectant and water. Do *not* mix ammonia and bleach. Wash every surface, under surfaces too." With that, Kennedy wandered off into the bunkhouse.

Jesus fucking Christ. The room looked like a warzone. To my right was Hal's mess. When Chasten had gotten up from the table, he'd knocked the bowl of coleslaw to the floor. It had shattered the glass and sent soggy cabbage and carrots flying in all directions. Kennedy had been right about the trail of breadcrumbs Ozzy had left.

In that moment, all I wanted to do was cry. I was overwhelmed and scared, with no idea of what I should tackle first. From where I was standing, I could hear Kennedy speaking, probably to the fire chief. Oh my God, was I really responsible for this?

There wasn't time to think about the ramifications of today. I was certain a shit storm was coming my way, but right now, I needed to clean up this room and do whatever I could to help the firehouse.

I figured the best place to start was with the floor. It sounded like Kennedy was calling out the troops so the floor needed to be clean for the people who might be running in or out. As quickly as I could, I snapped on a pair of gloves and grabbed the bucket I used to wash the engines. While it was filling up, it gave me a few minutes to figure out just how the hell to clean up puke. I gagged in my mouth just thinking about it. There would be time to sympathy puke later.

Thankfully there was no mess downstairs, but I did use my disinfectant bucket to wipe down the handrail leading to the second floor. Once I was back upstairs, I started with the coleslaw, locating the broken pieces of the bowl and using a sponge and the dustpan to clean it up.

Moving around the other side of the table, I contemplated Hal's mess. I felt so bad for the young EMT. He'd been nothing but kind to me and I may have killed him. I took a deep breath and got to work. Ten minutes later, the floor was clean.

"Gunnar?" a familiar female voice called up the stairs.

Thank Christ the cavalry was here. I would know that voice anywhere. It was Mandy McCoy. "In the kitchen," I called back.

I wasn't prepared for what came up the stairs. Mandy was wearing a pair of bright yellow kitchen gloves and carrying bags from Target. "Are you okay?" She rushed to me, stopping a few feet shy of me and seemed to be looking me over.

"Yeah, but the others." I felt my emotions rising to the top again.

Without hesitation, Mandy closed the distance between us and hugged me close.

"Ah, Jesus, Mom. You're hugging the enemy," Kennedy said from the bunkhouse door.

"The enemy? What is wrong with you?" Mandy sounded angry.

Kennedy point an accusatory finger at me. "Gunnar was the one who cooked for everyone today."

"So then why isn't he sick too?" Mandy released me and took aim at her son. "Why aren't you sick? Don't you dare tell me you sat at the table and watched everyone else eat. I know you better than that."

Kennedy's cheeks colored. "No, Gunnar isn't sick. Neither am I." His tone indicated he hadn't given a second thought to that fact before his mother brought it up. "I did eat the ribs. They were top-notch until…" Kennedy left the rest of that thought unsaid.

"Until you were at ground zero of a barf-o-rama?" Mandy's eyes glittered with amusement.

Kennedy grimaced. "Yeah, something like that."

"Were you here yesterday?" Mandy asked me. "Did you have contact with Ozzy or any of the other firefighters or EMTs?"

"No. My last shift was Friday and I spent yesterday catching up on my sleep." I chanced a look at Kennedy. He wore a serious look on his face, but he didn't look angry anymore.

"Shame on you, Kennedy, for making this poor boy feel like he's to blame for this. Stomach bug symptoms usually start showing up twelve to twenty-four hours after coming in contact with the virus. Since neither of you were here yesterday, it makes sense you're both still standing." She winked at me before turning back to Kennedy. "Now, get out of here. Your father and I will take care of everyone else and we'll be here when the chief shows up. If he shows up." Mandy grimaced. "I've never met a man in my life with as sensitive a stomach as Chief Higgins. Both of you. Out."

"I'll go as soon as I've cleaned this mess up." The rest of the food still needed to be thrown away and the dishes, pots and pans needed scrubbing.

"David and I will take care of everything. Now scoot." She set a gloved hand against my face. "If you need anything, you call us. Got it?" I managed a weak nod. Much more than that and I would be sobbing. There was no way I could thank her enough for everything she'd done for me today. "Tell Ozzy I hope he feels better."

"You'll tell him yourself when you come back to work." Mandy's voice was sweet, but she'd leveled an angry look at Kennedy.

No one had to tell me twice to leave. I gave Mandy one last smile and booked it down the stairs like I'd stolen something.

Today had been the most perfect day of my life. Until the barf-o-rama.

15

Kennedy

Several hours later I felt sick to my stomach. Not because I was coming down with whatever had wiped out Ozzy and the firehouse, but because I'd been such a dick to Gunnar.

Mom had insisted I go home so that I wouldn't come in contact with whatever it was making them so sick, but the damage was done. I'd been there for the better part of five hours. Chances were pretty high that I had touched a contaminated surface and there was the hug Ozzy gave me that lasted at least thirty seconds. He'd also whispered in my ear. I figured I was fucked either way. It wouldn't hurt for me to stick around and give my parents a hand while I was still upright and didn't have my head in the toilet.

Chief Higgins closed Firehouse Three until the contagion was under control. Who the hell used words like *contagion*? He didn't want anyone who'd been in the firehouse to come in contact with the other three houses in town. It was bad timing with an arsonist on the loose. The rest of the department would pull together and get things done. This was their city. They'd protect it at all costs.

Everyone, with the exception of Ozzy, had gotten home safely. He'd insisted on staying at the firehouse. It hadn't been unmanned since it had been opened in February of 1941. The house had stayed manned through the bombing of Pearl Harbor ten months later, through dozens of hurricanes, and on America's darkest day, September 11th. Ozzy wasn't about to let the stomach bug end seventy-nine years of tradition.

I'd been torn between staying with my stubborn-ass brother or going home to check on to my stubborn-ass neighbor. How the hell had I ended up surrounded by so many mule-headed asshats? That wasn't a question I wanted to delve into very deeply. I had a feeling I was the lowest common denominator in the equation.

Ozzy assured me that he was going to be fine. Since he was the only person staying at the firehouse, he wouldn't have to share the bathroom with anyone. I'd finally left when he promised to call me if he thought he needed to be taken to the ER. He may have also mentioned a time or two that Gunnar would be all alone if I stayed at the firehouse with him.

Driving home, I started thinking about the apology I owed Gunnar. I'd come right out and accused him of poisoning the entire firehouse. Shit, what a complete and total asshole I'd been to him. I think part of the reason for my dickery had to do with the fact that I was attracted to this boy and I didn't want to be.

I was single. *Happily* single. There was no need to upset my carefully stacked applecart with a boy who was practically half my age. Okay, maybe I was exaggerating a tiny bit. He was twenty-one and I was thirty. But there was the fact that he'd grown up with a platinum spoon in his mouth. In my book growing up like that made Gunnar younger than his years. At least that's what I kept telling myself. I think it had to do with him never having dealt with hard times or strife the way I had.

In a way, that made me sound like an elitist tragedy asshole. No one's childhood could have possibly been worse than my own. Of course, what Ozzy and Dallas went through came pretty damn close. Regardless of how Gunnar's life had gone, he'd never seen his mother's murdered body, he'd never been beaten and scarred for life by his father, and he hadn't been left alone for days at a time while his mother whored herself for drugs, like my brothers and I had.

Thinking that way made me feel sick to my stomach. I guess I wasn't fit for human company tonight. Or any night, really. If I was being completely honest with myself that was the reason I was single. My mother couldn't live without a man. I'd be damned if I was going to follow in her footsteps. I'd rather be alone than be with a man who'd treat me the way her boyfriends treated her.

I was being completely over the top in the drama department. It was the only place in my life where the terror of my childhood poked through the carefully crafted man I'd become. I'd only ever been to therapy, as an adult, when the police department mandated it. We'd lost a colleague in the line of duty three years ago. I wasn't a stupid man. I knew what to say when the inevitable comparison to my mother came up in the course of that session.

I wasn't stupid and I wasn't primed to be the victim either. I'd started working out early. Ozzy and Dallas had been quick to join me. We never said the words out loud to each other, but I knew we were all bulking up so no one could ever hurt us again.

That's also one of the reasons I became a cop. When you were six foot, 3 inches tall and carried a gun for a living, there weren't many people who wanted to fuck with me, professionally at least.

When it came to the bedroom, that was another story. I'd done my fair share of fucking around. Who hasn't? The difference between me and other, normal men, is that the second I started feeling anything at all for the guy I was banging, I was out the door.

Over the years I'd kept up with the scientific literature on kids who'd grown up in homes like I lived in with my mother or who grew up in foster care. We all seemed to fall into two categories: people who would do anything for love to avoid living like they did as kids and people like me and my brothers who would do anything to avoid love. It wasn't a coincidence that all three of us were in our thirties and hadn't settled down yet.

All of the lights were blazing in Gunnar's house when I pulled into my driveway. I'd noticed they always were. It made me wonder if he was afraid of the dark. Not that I was going to come out and ask him. I had a feeling he was afraid of everything right now, including me. He had a right to be after the way I shouted at him earlier. I really was a dick.

Unfortunately, there was nothing I could do about that sorry state of affairs at the moment. I climbed my stairs and let myself into the house. It was cool and quiet. I hated that. I'd thought about getting myself a dog or a cat but couldn't seem to commit to a pet either. What scared me the most was that the animal had an expiration date. I wasn't sure I could deal with loving and then losing something I absolutely cherished. My mind was one rocky-ass minefield tonight.

After a cool shower, I felt more human, but I was worn to the bone. I'd wanted to jack off in the shower but didn't even have the energy for that. I hoped I wasn't coming down with the puking bug. That was the last thing I needed. I couldn't help thinking about my parents willingly exposing themselves to the biohazard. My mom had been in the men's room rubbing backs while the guys hurled. Just like she'd done with us as kids.

I'd like to think I have that kind of empathy in me, that my early experiences don't completely define who I am as a man.

When I was dried off and dressed in a clean pair of boxers, I spotted my phone on the nightstand. I hit the home button and no one had called or texted while I was in the shower. My mind turned again to Gunnar. Was he okay? Had he gotten infected by the stomach bug. Was he suffering? Sleeping?

After the way I treated him today, he sure in hell wasn't going to call me if he were in trouble. Knowing I could regret this later, I grabbed my phone and called him before I could think better of it. Gunnar's line rang and rang. Just when I was about to hang up, a weak voice answered, "Hello?"

"Gunnar? It's Kennedy. Are you okay?" Christ had I just woken him up or was he sick?

"Dying, I think," he muttered and gagged.

I would know that sound anywhere. "I'll be right over. Can you unlock the door for me?"

"Hate me," Gunnar half-whispered.

"Don't be ridiculous. Open the door." I hung up without waiting for him to answer. Quickly throwing on a pair of jeans and a t-shirt, I hustled out of my room and downstairs. Twisting my feet into my sneakers, I grabbed my keys and was out the door.

My heart was pounding in my chest and it wasn't from my sprint down the stairs and out the door. How long had he been sick? I knew he was upset with me, but why hadn't he called my mother?

When I got to the top of his front steps, I tried the door. It was still locked. "Gunnar, it's me. Open the door." My stomach ached with worry. What if he'd passed out with his head in the toilet bowl? I wasn't above grabbing a sledgehammer and pounding my way into the house if it came down to that. Just as I was trying to remember where I'd put my hammer, the door opened a crack.

"Holy shit!" I said under my breath. I'd seen dead people who looked better than Gunnar did. "You look awful."

"*And* the horse you rode in on." Gunnar gagged, his hands slapping over his mouth as he took off running for the bathroom.

Maybe that hadn't been the best opening line of my life. I let myself into the house and locked the door behind me. Even with the door shut, I could hear Gunnar retching. I took a deep breath through my mouth and followed him.

I was about to knock on the bathroom door when I heard Gunnar start to cry. In that moment, my heart broke for him. He was sick and alone with no family here to support him. All he had was me. My gut instinct told me to barge in there and force him to believe everything was going to be all right. Before I made a bigger mess of things, I stopped and thought about how Mandy would handle this. She would have known Gunnar needed a gentler touch. It wasn't my stock in trade, but I would do my best.

Rapping a knuckle against the door, I let myself into the bathroom. Gunnar was on his knees with his face resting against the toilet seat. I hit the flush valve and grabbed a clean washcloth. I couldn't help snickering.

"What the fuck could possibly be funny in this moment?" Gunnar didn't bother to raise his head. "Poetic justice that I poisoned everyone at the station and now I'm in the same boat?"

I dipped the soft cloth under the cool water tap before kneeling beside him. "No, silly boy. I have these exact towels in my house. So do Ozzy, Hennessey, and Dallas. My mom was always in the habit of buying us boys the exact same things so none of us could say the other was her favorite."

"Yeah, okay. You're just glad this thing bit me in the ass too."

"No, I'm not. I'm so sorry I said that to you. I'm a total asshole. Sometimes I talk before I think and I was just so worried about my brother and the rest of the firehouse. I needed someone to blame because I couldn't save any of them. I picked you. Can you ever forgive me?"

Gunnar nodded, looking more miserable now than he had when he answered the door.

Silent tears poured out of Gunnar's eyes as I wiped his sweaty face down. He definitely had a fever. I hung the cloth on the rack and scooped Gunnar into my arms. "There was this one Christmas, it was my second with the McCoys. The *in* toy that year was those stuffed dogs. Pound Puppies, I think they were called. Mom got all four of us different dogs and oh man did we fight!" I snorted. "We fought so much, we ruined Christmas."

"Ruined Christmas?" Gunnar's voice was weak.

I set Gunnar down on the bed. "My mom took the four dogs and shut herself in her room." I would never forget that Christmas as long as I lived. "David sat the four of us down on the couch and paced in front of us without saying a word. We all burst into tears from the guilt."

"Poor Mandy. Did you manage to be a hero and save Christmas?"

I'd never thought of myself as a hero, especially since I'd been part of the reason Christmas had been ruined in the first place. "We all were heroes, I guess. All four of us headed to my mother's bedroom and peeked in the door. She was sitting on the side of the bed with her head in her hands. Our little stuffed dogs were lined up at the front of the bed looking like they were going to jump off. We all grabbed the dog we'd been given and climbed over Mandy, making sad puppy sounds and rubbing the dogs against her face and arms. She started laughing and Christmas was saved."

Gunnar was looking at me like I hung the moon. My stomach twisted with the ramifications of that look. There wasn't time to think about it now, not with him being so sick. "Can I get you anything?"

"Another cool cloth?" Gunnar offered a week smile.

"Sure thing. I'll be right back."

"My guardian angel," he whispered as I walked toward the bathroom.

I didn't believe that for a minute. Gunnar must have a higher fever than I thought.

16

Gunnar

I wanted to die. Not in a melodramatic, tell-my-mother-I-love-her way, but literally. My entire body ached, even my hair. My teeth felt funny in my gums and I kept going back and forth between feeling like I'd been left on an arctic ice floe to stuck in an oven set to char-broil. Death was preferable to all that, and so much more.

What was worse than all these things combined was the dream I had. In it, Kennedy was here seeing to my every need. He put cool cloths on my head and did his best to keep me warm or cool depending on my circumstance. He'd even told me stories about growing up in the McCoy house. It was all a dream. When I woke up a few seconds ago, Mandy McCoy was sitting with me, reading a Harlequin Romance novel.

"Kennedy?" My eyes felt like they were glued together. I was too weak to open them all the way.

"No, honey, it's Mandy." Her full attention was on me, as was her right hand checking for a fever. "You're still running warm."

Hearing Mandy confirm Kennedy wasn't here confirmed my suspicion that what I'd had was a very vivid dream. Damn it. That scene with Kennedy's apology and him carrying me to bed were the only things I'd had that made this situation worthwhile.

"I sent him out to get something to eat and shower, sweetie. Kennedy said he'd be back later. I don't think he slept last night." Mandy wore a frown.

"You mean he really was here? I didn't hallucinate him?" Kennedy stayed awake all night? No, that couldn't possibly be true. Could it?

"No, he was really here. Wouldn't leave your side even though I was afraid he'd catch this bug from you." Mandy fussed with the tangled sheet around my middle. I couldn't even remember my own mother doing anything like this for me.

Now wasn't the time to think about that. I'd been out of the house for a month and there hadn't been any contact from my mother at all. It was like I was truly dead to her. "How did you and David decide to become foster parents?"

The surprised look on Mandy's face made me think I'd made a mistake in asking her. Shock quickly turned to surprise. "Hennessey was the light of my life. My little boy was everything to me." Her eyes had gone misty.

Never in my life had my mother ever said anything like that about me. I was a lot of things, but not the light of her life. I was worried about where this story was going. Could Mandy not have any other biological children?

"There was a boy in his kindergarten class named Jimmy. He was the sweetest little boy. Blond with blue eyes and a missing front tooth. When he met people he'd grab on to your pant leg and smile up at you." A lone tear slid down her cheek. "His mother was selling herself to finance her drug habit and his father was out of the picture, if he'd ever been in it at all."

I had a sinking feeling in the pit of my stomach. This wasn't going to end well. I wasn't sure I wanted to hear how it ended, but I had to. "What happened?" My voice was barely above a whisper.

"Jimmy found his mother's drug stash when she was sleeping off a bender." Mandy swiped at the tears flowing down her face. "He died alone on the dirty floor of his mother's double wide."

My own emotions were out of control. That poor boy.

"Division of Children and Family Services had been out to the trailer half a dozen times in the two short months Jimmy had been enrolled in school. They should have taken him from the house, but they didn't." Mandy straightened her spine as she took a deep breath. "Even if they had, David and I were in no position to bring another child into our home at the spur of the moment. I went to the library the next day while Hennessey was in school and I grabbed every book I could find on being a foster parent. David and I went out and furnished the spare bedroom with twin beds. Then we were approved as foster parents. A month later, we got our first child, Quentin. His mother had been in a similar situation to Jimmy's. Only, she turned her life around. He lived with us for three years while his mother got her life back together. I hated giving him back but returning the child to the bio parent is always their goal."

"Is he okay?" I was still gobsmacked by the story Mandy had told me.

"We see him all the time. He's a life flight pilot. As Quentin got older, he chose to come stay with us. Got himself emancipated and spent his high school years in our home. Those were the best times of my life, having my five boys in the house. They nearly ate me and David out of house and home, but it was worth it." Her eyes were misty again, but this time from joy rather than sorrow. "Being a mom is what I was born to do."

"Is that why you're being so kind to me?" Did she see me as some poor little orphan boy?

Mandy's head shifted to the side. She seemed to be studying me. "You're a special young man, Gunnar. Being a mom might be what I was born to do, but it doesn't mean that every mother feels the same way. You might have hit the jackpot with your parents having money, but that doesn't mean you hit the parent jackpot."

Wasn't that the truth. "I can't thank you enough for looking after me and telling Kennedy that everyone getting sick wasn't my fault."

That thoughtful look came back into her blue eyes. "Do you know the story about what happened to Kennedy's real mother?"

As far as I was concerned, Mandy was his *real* mother, but I wasn't going to give voice to those words. I nodded instead.

"Kennedy felt like her death was his fault."

"His fault?" Okay, maybe I hadn't heard the entire story.

Mandy reached out to brush a stray lock of hair off my face. "He doesn't tell the story very often. It took me three years before he would tell me what wasn't in the police report."

"That sounds like Kennedy." Stubborn to his core.

"The last fight started over Kennedy not having done his homework. He was watching a television show and was going to get to it when it ended. The mother's boyfriend took exception to that and hit him. For the first time in her life, Kitty stood up to her boyfriend, so he went after her instead. When she was dead, he came after Kennedy. Thankfully, the police burst through the door before anything else could happen to him. He landed on my doorstep a few hours later. I knew from the moment I set eyes on him that he was meant to be my son."

Damn, that was one hell of a story. "How long did it take for Kennedy to realize the same thing?" I knew it hadn't happened overnight.

"It was the night he finally told me what happened when his mother was killed. He'd just turned thirteen and we'd been having some behavioral problems with him acting out. We took him to see a counselor so that he would have someone to help him sort out his feelings. What he told us a few weeks later was that he couldn't save his mother. All these years later and he felt guilt that he'd been the catalyst that led to her death."

Damn. I sat with those words for a few seconds. I wasn't the sharpest tool in the drawer when it came to human relationships, but I could see the reason for Kennedy blowing up at me yesterday. "His brother was sick and there was nothing he could do to make that go away, so he yelled at the person he thought caused the situation. Me."

"I think that has a lot to do with it. Once Kennedy realized he had a true family, he became fiercely loyal to all of us and the other foster kids who drifted in and out of our house over the years. Once you were part of Kennedy's pack, you were in it for life, so to speak. We had a few issues with him being a bit," Mandy paused, obviously searching for the right word, "overzealous."

I managed to snicker. "Yeah, I can see that about him. How is Ozzy doing this morning?"

Mandy's face lit up with a bright smile. "He's better. Still running a bit of a fever and was looking a little green, but he's going to be just fine. It will be a cold day in hell when a stomach bug brings down my stubborn boy."

"Talking about me behind my back, Mom?" Kennedy asked from the bedroom door.

His sudden appearance scared the hell out of me. I hadn't heard him come back in the house or climb the stairs.

"Of course not, sweetheart." She rolled her eyes. "Gunnar asked how Ozzy was doing this morning and I was telling him that my stubborn son was better. I can see where you thought I was talking about you." Mandy set a hand on my shoulder. "Try some small sips of water. I know you'll feel the urge to chug it, but don't. You don't want it going out through the in door. I'll check on you later. Sleep if you need to." Mandy hugged Kennedy and was gone.

"You're looking better this morning." Kennedy took the chair his mother had vacated.

"I feel like I was hit by a bus." Kennedy looked amazing. His dirty-blond hair was damp and I could smell his fresh soap. If I didn't know better, I'd guess he was in a hurry to get back here. To me. Shit, I must still have a fever to be having thoughts like that.

"Ozzy said the same thing when I spoke to him this morning. He's on the mend though. So are the rest of the guys." Kennedy gave his shoulder a careless shrug.

"I thought I'd hallucinated the whole thing." I could feel the color rising high on my cheeks. I was hoping Kennedy would think it was the fever coming back.

"What whole thing? Me being here to save your ass last night?" His lips curved into a drop-dead sexy grin.

"It wasn't my ass that needed saving." At least, not in the beginning. That part came later.

"I knew Ozzy would be all right by himself. He'd call my parents if things were worse than he could handle. You, on the other hand, needed me." Kennedy's blue eyes went wide. Obviously, he hadn't meant to let that slip.

My heart sang at those words. Of course I needed him. Wanted him. After he'd blamed me for poisoning the firehouse, I wasn't about to tell him that. I was still going to hold that close to my heart. I took a different tact instead. "I did need you. If you hadn't shown up, I would have spent the night with my head resting on the toilet seat."

Kennedy snorted before a serious look overcame his features. "I'm glad you're feeling better."

"I'm glad you didn't get this thing. It's pretty fucking miserable." That was no word of a lie.

"Do what my mom said. Take baby sips. Sleep when you need to."

"It's Monday. My shift at the firehouse starts in two hours. I need to be there for my team." I'd almost said family. I was going to keep that to myself as well.

"Are you kidding me? Twelve hours ago, you were knocking on heaven's door. You're not going to work today, and neither are the other guys. Ozzy is there already, but I swear he's superhuman." Kennedy got up from his seat. He pressed a quick kiss to my forehead. "Feel better. I'll text you later."

"Be safe," I called out after him.

I could feel the ghost of his kiss on my forehead long after he'd left.

17

Kennedy

Two hours later, I was still on edge, after hearing my mother tell Gunnar the story of how she and David decided to become foster parents. It had been eighteen years since I'd heard the story for the first time and it never failed to bring me to my knees.

It was the last Friday of spring break. Mandy had been home with the four of us while David went to work. We were all going on a two-week family vacation to the Grand Canyon in the summer, so David didn't have any vacation days to use in April.

Looking back on it now, my brothers and I were awful that week. It had rained for five days straight and all we wanted to do was get outside and see our friends or ride bikes, but we couldn't. Mom didn't want us to have any other kids over. None of us understood why at the time. Now, of course, we all knew it was because there would be witnesses if she killed one or all of us.

I don't remember what started this particular fight, maybe Ozzy does since he's the oldest. All I remember was that it ended with the four of us shouting, "You're not my real brother!" then the fists started to fly.

When our mom arrived on the scene, Hennessy had me pinned face down on the floor with my left arm twisted behind my back, slamming my face against the floor. Dallas had a bloody nose and Ozzy had a black eye coming on.

Even though my brains were a bit scrambled, I'll never forget the look on Mandy's face when she saw us beating the crap out of each other. She looked devastated. The only other time I've seen that look on her face was when foster kids had been removed from our house. She sat down on the floor across from us and shouted, "Boys!"

That one word stopped us all in our tracks. I remember thinking this was it. This would be the moment when she'd call my case worker and tell her to come get me. I could see Ozzy from my spot on the floor and he looked terrified. It was the only time in my life I'd ever seen that look on his face. He thought there would be trouble too. We'd all gone too far.

Hennessey climbed off my back and pulled me up. Ozzy sat on one side of me, with Dallas on the other. While we all moved around, I'd been mentally preparing myself to face my doom.

"So, you're not *real* brothers, huh?" Mandy had asked quietly. Her eyes moved to each of us in turn. I remember my eyes were burning with unshed tears. "You stand up for each other when one of you gets bullied. There are hugs when one of you is going through something. Late night talks after lights out when you share your heart and your fears. If these things don't make you brothers, what are you?"

No one had answered, but I'd heard Ozzy gasp in obvious surprise.

"You boys are my sons. Not *fake* sons. *Real* sons." Her blue eyes glittered with conviction. "The only thing fake in this room is my hair color."

Dallas barked out a quick laugh before he clapped his hands over his mouth.

"No, it's funny alright." Mandy shrugged her dainty shoulders. "Brothers fight, boys. That's normal. It's healthy to disagree and then come back together to figure out how to resolve the issue. What isn't healthy, and what I won't tolerate, are the four of you saying you're not real brothers. Call each other assclowns if you like, but I don't ever want to hear you say that again."

All four of us laughed hysterically. Mandy never said bad words and assclown was the funniest thing I'd ever heard.

After we finished laughing, all four of us mobbed her with hugs and kisses. After everything calmed down, she told us the story about Jimmy and becoming foster parents. Tears slipped down her cheeks when she told us that she would have saved him if she'd only known how.

She'd left the room after that and we all apologized to each other. Ozzy had shocked me by telling the story about his scar and how he'd ended up on the McCoy's doorstep. Dallas went next. Then me. Hennessy talked about what it was like to learn what being dead meant.

In that moment I realized other kids had lives that were as bad or worse than my own. I'd never heard the others tell their own backstories before and they crushed me. Even at twelve years old, I'd had the empathy to put myself in my brothers' shoes. I made a vow to myself that when I was older, I was going to protect people like myself and my brothers. I guess the others had the same idea.

Ozzy became a fireman, Dallas an EMT, and then there was Hennessey's failed attempt at being a dispatcher. To be honest, it didn't fail so much as die a quick, painful death. In his own way, Hen was helping people with the bar, even if his soul was paying the price.

My ringing phone startled me out of my memories. It was Ozzy. "Hey, man."

"Hey there yourself. How's your boy doing?" I could hear the snark in Ozzy's voice.

"He's not my boy," I protested weakly. "He's better. Still has a fever and the chills. Gunnar is trying to drink little sips of water and he's stopped *going*." Shit, maybe I didn't need to give Ozzy that much detail.

"Yeah, he's not your boy, but you know more specifics about his health than his doctor." There was a laugh in his voice.

"How are you feeling?" I needed to change the subject and fast. The last thing I wanted to do was go down the Gunnar rabbit hole with him.

"I'm not going to run a marathon today."

I couldn't help laughing. "Let's be honest, you're not going to run a marathon any other day either."

"Assclown!" Ozzy shot back.

"Takes one to know one," I sneered back, sounding like I did when I was twelve. "I'm on my way to see Ella before heading to work. Do you need anything? Gatorade? Toilet paper?"

"I could use Gatorade and water. Mom isn't available to drop by for a few more hours. I wonder why that is?" Ozzy's snark was back in full force.

Ozzy obviously knew why our mother wasn't available. "Mom's with Gunnar."

"Uh, huh. But he's *not* your boy."

"Mom's been looking out for strays longer than we've both known her. Gunnar is just another in a long line."

"Bullshit! I saw the way you were looking at each other yesterday before the hurling started. There was a lot of eyelash batting and sighing. I was about to lose my lunch watching it."

"You did lose your lunch." I couldn't help laughing again. "More than once, if memory serves." I was giving him shit in hopes he'd stop talking about the way I was looking at Gunnar. Leave it to Ozzy to have noticed. I wonder if any of the others had noticed too.

What I was interested in was the way Gunnar had been looking at me. The problem was that I didn't want Ozzy to know.

"Funny, asshole. Just for that, I'm not going to tell you how Gunnar was looking at you."

Ozzy always did know exactly what I was thinking. "Good! I didn't want to know anyway." But I did. I really did.

"Uh, huh," Ozzy drawled. "I want the blue Gatorade and a box o' soup." Ozzy's voice had lost its snark. Now he just sounded tired.

"The kind with the circle noodles. I know." Ozzy's drug of choice when he was sick was Lipton Noodle O's soup. I'd been planning on getting him some of that anyway with apple sauce and some crackers. Come to think of it, Gunnar could use some of that too. I'd drop his stuff off during my meal break.

"In case this thing kills me, I love you, little brother." Ozzy was definitely tapped out.

"Love you too." I hung up before Ozzy got more emotional. I'd seen the same kind of emotions from Gunnar this morning. Being sick made people vulnerable. At least the kid had my mom there to take care of him.

It had been a long night with Gunnar. I'd moved the television from the living room to the bedroom so we could watch *Lego Masters* until he fell asleep. After he nodded off, I couldn't help staring at him to make sure he was still breathing. If I had a nickel for every time I took his temperature, I could retire. My mother showing up earlier this morning to spell me was a Godsend. The longer I sat with Gunnar, the more I had to admit I liked him.

I might have been calling him a boy in my mind, but the way he'd kissed me the other night was all man. I supposed the biggest question, at the moment, was if I wanted to explore that further. I wouldn't wish illness on Gunnar, but I did have to admit it gave me time to think about what I wanted to do next.

18

Gunnar

A week later, everything was back to normal. Firehouse Three was healthy again and no one held any ill will against me. I think the fact that one of them gave me this bug made them all see me in a different light.

Thankfully, I'd gotten over the harsher symptoms in two days. I still felt like a wet dishrag but got my raggedy ass out of bed to go to work. I can't say it was all fun and games, but I got the job done.

Not that I was thinking about the outbreak or who gave it to me now. Today would be the day my dream to go on a ride along with the firehouse would come true. If someone's house caught on fire, that was. Shit, saying it like that made me sound like an asshole.

Ozzy had pulled me into this office when I'd gotten to the station and let me know the chief had granted his request to let me come along on a call. Of course, in order for that to happen, there needed to be a fire or an accident that required an attending engine. I also had to sign an ass load of paperwork stating I wouldn't sue the department or the city of Gloucester if anything happened to me. There were also equipment waivers to sign too, saying I wouldn't use any of it.

I practically danced out of Ozzy's office. A month ago, I never would have given a thought to going out on a call with any branch of emergency services. To tell the truth, before I met Kennedy, I'd never really given much of a thought to the men and women who kept me safe.

It was pretty humbling, to think that someone like Ozzy had been there for me without me ever having to return the favor. How did people become that selfless? In my entire life, I don't think I've ever done anything for the good of someone else, unless there was something in it for me.

So far as I could tell, what was in it for Ozzy, Hal, Chasten, or any of the others never crossed their minds. For that matter neither did their own personal safety.

When I set my house on fire a few weeks back, I'd been terrified. Literally scared shitless. I remember freezing when I saw the flames shooting up from the frying pan. In that moment, I didn't know what to do or how to save myself or my home. Finally, some kind of lizard-brain instinct kicked in and I ran outside.

My first instinct had been to run out of the burning building. How on earth did running into a burning building become Ozzy's first instinct? Was it something David and Mandy taught him? Or was it part of his DNA like his dark hair and eyes?

Maybe when this was over, I'd ask him. The same for Kennedy. I mean, hell, that man could have bullets flying at his head at any moment, just like that day with Ella. It could have so easily been Kennedy who took the bullet that day in the shitty motel room. Christ, what the hell would I have done if it had been Kennedy?

I couldn't breathe thinking about it. My knees knocked together, and I felt my vision starting to grey out at the edges.

"Hey, Noob! You gonna help me inventory the rig or are you gonna stand there all day with your head in the clouds?"

I snapped out of my mental nervous breakdown to see Hal grinning at me. He'd mentioned doing inventory on the ambulance when I'd gotten in. I'd promised to help but visualizing Kennedy's corpse on the floor of a shitty motel room chased any other thought away. "Coming."

"You'd know if you were coming." Hal snorted as I climbed into the back of the ambulance. Now that I knew my way around it a bit, it fascinated me. There were so many drawers and compartments to keep various kinds of supplies and drugs.

"You finally feeling back to your old self." It wasn't a question. Hal's usually creamy skin had a greenish pallor to it all week. Today was the first day he looked like his old self.

"I think so. It's my strength that's taking the longest to come back." He had a clipboard on his lap and was peering into the drawer with gauze in it. "Here, you take this, and I'll call out numbers to you."

Dutifully, I wrote down the numbers of supplies in the bus. There was a time or two when I had no damn clue what the hell he was talking about, but Hal was always happy to take a minute and explain the item and what it was used for in the field.

"What the hell were you thinking about earlier? You looked like you were having a mental meltdown."

Leave it to Hal to have noticed my distress. "I was thinking about Kennedy's family."

A bit of the bright light in Hal's eyes dimmed. "I see."

"Three of those brothers decided that running into danger while everyone else was running away was how they wanted to spend their lives. I was just wondering where that comes from?" It wasn't a surprise to me that Hal had a bit of a crush. He was the nicest man I'd ever met in my life and if I'd met him first instead of Kennedy, things might have been different.

"When I was a teenager, my best friend and I were riding our dirt bikes home one night. It was dark and we were late getting home. When I called home to tell my Dad what was going on, he offered to come pick us up. I said no because I didn't want him to leave the house in addition to him being pissed that I missed curfew. We rounded a bend on this back-country road and there was a car heading straight for us. It was on the opposite side of the yellow line. I remember shouting for Tim to get out of the way, but the car hit him. If I live to be a hundred, I'll never forget the sight of him hitting the hood of the car and bouncing off its roof."

"Sweet Jesus," I gasped. What an awful thing to have seen. I didn't want to know how the story ended, but I needed to. "What did you do?"

"I called 911. Told them where we were and what happened. While we waited for help to arrive, I sat by Tim, holding his hand and telling him everything was going to be okay. I didn't know how that was possible. His legs were twisted into an impossible position and even in the low light, I could see his bone sticking out."

"Oh my God." I'd seen shit like that on television, but the idea of seeing it in real life, and the injured person being a friend of mine, was beyond anything I could imagine.

"I thought he was going to die." Hal's eyes shimmered with unshed tears. "When help arrived, there were two ambulances. One crew started to help Tim, while the other went to the man who'd crashed his car into us. It had never crossed my mind to go see if he was okay."

Okay, so running into danger to help people wasn't something Hal was born with. Although, I couldn't help thinking if the roles were reversed, I wouldn't have given a fuck about what happened to the man who hit my friend. "It wouldn't have crossed my mind either."

"That was my first lesson in life-saving. You don't get to choose whose life to save. You save them all. Sinner. Saint. Best friend. Mortal enemy." The look on Hal's face was unreadable. He seemed lost in his memories.

I kept my mouth shut, not wanting to interrupt.

"Turned out the guy was drunk, and he didn't have a scratch on him. Making matters worse was this wasn't his first DUI. I should have been watching what was going on with Tim, but I'd been mesmerized by the police pulling him out of the car and making him do a field sobriety test." Hal gave his head a shake. "Dirty fucker." He looked back up at me with brighter eyes. "The real action was what the paramedics were doing with Tim. They'd gotten his neck protected and his legs straightened out. I'd been right, his bone was sticking out. Compound fracture of his tibia and fibula. What struck me the hardest was that he wasn't screaming. There was a paramedic at his head speaking to him softly."

"Max told me you do something similar on calls." I grinned at him. I was a big fan of Max.

Hal blushed. "Max has a big mouth."

Maxine Smithfield was Hal's partner on the ambulance. She was in her mid-forties and loved her job more than her life. If there was ever an extra shift that needed to be taken, or if someone had been assigned to work a holiday or important birthday, Max was always the one to take the shift, no questions asked. "Maybe she does, but I'm guessing you wanted to be just like the paramedic who'd helped Tim that day."

His face turned a brighter shade of red. "I did. He was cute as hell, but it was the way he took care of Tim. That wreck was the worst thing I'd seen in my life, but that medic spoke to him like all he had was a skinned knee. Not only did Tim live, but he regained full function. We were out riding bikes again in six months."

"You wanted to help others conquer their fear." It was a noble sentiment, that was for sure. I'd never given a thought to that in my life. Until I met Kennedy and his family, no one had ever soothed my fears either. Damn, it was a hell of day for self-realization.

"We're all set here. Thanks for your help."

"No worries." I set a hand on Hal's shoulder and gave it a squeeze. I could tell he needed a bit of time to himself.

I was halfway to the men's room when the bell rang announcing a call.

"Load up!" Ozzy shouted, running from his office.

Just like I'd done that night in my kitchen, I froze. The entire firehouse was in motion and I was standing there like a slug. Firefighters ran past me to get into their turnout gear. Maxine ran down the stairs, while Chasten used the firepole.

"You coming, Noob? Or are you going to stand there with your thumb up your ass?" Ozzy wore a grin I'd never seen on his face before.

I took off running for the hook and ladder truck. It took me a few valuable seconds to figure out how to haul myself into the cab. Chasten was pulling it out the bay door before I'd even shut my door. I over balanced and almost tumbled out. A huge hand on my back stopped me. I turned to see Ozzy laughing like a maniac as he held me back.

"Jesus Christ, kid, shut the door and buckle up!" He didn't stop laughing.

Once I was settled in, Duke handed me a headset. Ozzy was explaining what kind of call we were going out to. Duke Marks had been with the Gloucester Fire Department for three years.

"Structure fire out on Langsford Road. Single family home, fully engulfed.

The faces around me were grim. It seemed they knew something I didn't. Since I was just along for the ride, I didn't want to ask.

"Sounds like The Scorcher is at it again," Duke leaned over to whisper. Carl Waters and Jenks Perkins nodded along.

Shit. I should have known that. I was going to need to keep better tabs on what was happening around my firehouse. I covered my grin with my left hand. It was funny how I considered the house and the people in it mine.

The roar of the engine and the squeal of the siren made it hard to concentrate. What I could see was that everyone around me had their game faces on. I had no doubt Max and Hal wore the same expressions in the ambulance behind us.

"Noob!" Ozzy shouted in my headset. "Remember the rules. Stay out of the way. Don't touch anything. No Facebook Live or any of that other shit. Got it?"

"10-4," I called back.

The entire crew broke up into laughter. Ozzy turned to look back at me. "Only the cops say that." His eyes were glittering with excitement. "Stay in the truck."

With those words he was turning around and getting out of the engine.

The dispatchers hadn't been exaggerating. The entire house was on fire. From where I was sitting, I could see glass glittering on the front lawn. The smell of the smoke was cloying, even from here.

"Help!" a woman's voice screamed. She was hanging out the window of the second floor.

Jesus Christ. There was a beehive of activity going on around me with members of the crew going for hoses and Ozzy barking out orders, but my attention was focused on the woman in the window. I couldn't see her face clearly from the smoke and the dark of night, but I could hear the terror in her voice.

While Ozzy and Chasten ran into the house, I got out of the truck. I slid down to the ground, with my eyes glued to the house.

"My daughters! Help my daughters!" the woman screamed.

Kids? There were kids trapped in the growing inferno. Sweet merciful Christ. I hadn't prayed in God knew how long, but I was praying now.

It felt like forever for Carl and Jenks to bring the hose around, even though I knew it had only been a minute or two at the most. They directed the hose and a gush of water flew toward the house. From where I was standing, I could hear Duke operating the ladder.

The woman was still screaming when a dark figure appeared in the front door. He looked larger than life. It wasn't until he stumbled outside that I could see there was another person across his shoulders. With all the gear and equipment, I couldn't tell if it was Chasten or Ozzy. I started forward intent on helping the person that had just been pulled out of the fire and to see if the fireman was okay, when I remembered what Ozzy told me. Stay put.

How the hell could I stay put when people needed help? My heart was pounding in my chest as Hal and Max raced forward to help the person pulled from the house. I hoped with all my strength that it was the mother, but she'd still been screaming in the window when this person was being carried out.

Hal lifted the person to their feet and together, he and Max moved him off toward the ambulance. I could tell from the build and height that it was a man. Probably the father. The fireman got back to his feet and I could finally see Coyne on the back of his jacket. It was Chasten.

My attention went back to the window where the woman had been screaming. She was no longer there. Was she all right? Maybe Ozzy had her and was on his way back outside.

I was sweating like crazy. The night was still in the eighties and from where I was standing on the street, I could feel the heat of the blast washing against my face. If I was fifty yards from the blaze, how hot must it be inside. I made a mental note to ask Ozzy later.

Suddenly, there was a rumble followed by a flash. I was thrown back against the engine and fell to the ground. When I lifted my head, it was spinning. Through blurry eyes, I could see the lawn was burning. I shut my eyes and sat back up. My stomach was tossing and turning like it had done when I had the stomach flu. When I was sure I wasn't going to throw up, I opened my eyes. The garage was leveled. What I thought was the yard burning were pieces of the house the blast had scattered.

I looked around to count the members of the team. I found them all, with the exception of Ozzy. Where the hell was he? Not still trapped in that house? "Ozzy!" I shouted. My throat hurt from the strain.

Chasten headed back toward the front door and disappeared inside.

Oh my God. What did I do? Should I call Kennedy? What about Mandy and David? What the hell should I do?

Sitting on the ground wasn't helping anyone. I got unsteadily to my feet. When I was sure I wasn't going to fall flat on my face, I moved toward the house. A large hand grabbed my arm and pulled me against his chest.

"Where the hell do you think you're going, Gunnar?"

Kennedy. I would know that voice anywhere. How the hell had he gotten here without me seeing him? When I turned around there were blue flashing lights all over the place. I wasn't sure how I missed their arrival. It didn't even matter at the moment. "Why are you just standing here. Your brother is in that building." I was nearly hysterical.

"Look at me, Gunnar." Kennedy's voice was soft. So soft that I needed to lean closer to hear him better.

"I am looking at you and you're standing still." Raw panic gripped my entire body. I could barely breathe.

"I'm not wearing any protective gear. I wouldn't get more than three steps into that house before the smoke took me down. Is that what you want, boy?" His hand came up to tilt my chin toward him.

"Fuck no!" I screamed in his face. "Ozzy! We have to save him. He's…"

Kennedy's blue eyes darkened. "He's what?"

With as emotional as I was, I managed to catch that spark of jealousy in his eyes. "He's like a brother to me. All he does is look out for me. If anything happened to him…" I couldn't finish that sentence.

"It's going to be okay. I promise." Kennedy looked like he meant those words.

"How can you say that? He's still trapped in that inferno."

Kennedy turned my entire body around. I could see something materializing out of the smoke and what used to be the front door. Two men stumbled out the door carrying what appeared to be laundry. Christ, was that the mother and her daughters?

"Stay here. I fucking mean it, Gunnar. Do not fucking move from this spot." Kennedy was gone, running toward Ozzy.

The rest of the team converged on the scene. Max and Hal were followed by the second ambulance team. The scene was a mass of movement and I couldn't tell what the hell I was seeing.

"Suzi!" a hoarse voice shouted. "Katy! Bella!" the voice shouted again.

Out of the corner of my eye I could see the man who'd been carried out of the house by Chasten moving toward the beehive of activity. I could see the team was trying to save the lives of the people he was shouting for. I started moving toward him, knowing this was the one thing I could do to help. As I moved, I could see Kennedy with Ozzy who was sitting up. Thank Christ.

I intercepted the man as he started moving across the lawn. "Let them do their jobs."

"That's my family!" the man wailed.

My heart broke for him. It wasn't a good sign if the paramedics weren't loading his family for transport. The last thing they needed was to have their efforts impeded by this man. "What's your name?"

"Dillon. Dillon McMasters and that's my wife, Suzi, and our daughters, Katy and Belle. They're only four and two years old. Save them. You have to save them." Dillon's eyes plead with mine.

"They're in good hands. The best thing we can do is stay out of the way."

Dillon and I watched as the medics continued to work on the family. Kennedy was hauling Ozzy to his feet. He was cradling his left arm against his chest. It was obvious Ozzy was hurt. Knowing my boss, the man wouldn't have his arm looked at until everyone else had been tended to.

Kennedy's eyes found my own across the yard. He gave his head a little shake. I knew then the absolute worst had happened. How the hell was I going to help Dillon through the worst day of his life?

One by one, the paramedics fell back. Blankets were brought out to cover the bodies. I could see Hal and Chasten were crying. Max stood with her eyes slammed shut, her face turned up to the sky.

"Why are they stopping?" Dillon shouted. "Why aren't you helping my family?" He broke free of my grip heading toward the covered bodies of his family.

Ozzy and Kennedy lumbered toward him.

I stood in shock as they grabbed him and tried to talk to him. Dillon screamed. It sounded like a wild animal. He hit the ground beside his wife's body, screaming her name and begging the medics to help her.

With tears tracking down my cheeks, I turned from the grieving father and the members of my team. I didn't want them to see my weakness.

19

Kennedy

I couldn't bear to put Gunnar in the back of my cruiser. He was crushed enough over what he'd seen at the McMasters fire scene. While we waited for the Essex County Medical Examiner to come for the bodies, I'd done some research on the house and its owners.

Dillon and Suzi McMasters had been married for ten years. Katy was four years old and Bella was two. Katy's favorite movie was *Beauty and the Beast*. She'd wanted to name her little sister after her favorite princess. My heart broke when Dillon told me that story. What broke worse was Gunnar.

I could see the absolutely devastated look on his face. He would never be the same after this night. What was worse was that I had no idea what to say to help him heal again.

Ozzy had a pretty gnarly looking burn on his left arm. Hal and Max had been the ones to transport him to Gloucester Mercy Hospital. No matter how severe the burn was, my mule-stubborn brother would be back at the station tomorrow. Ozzy had been sure this was another arson.

There was too much going on for me to wrap my head around. Chief among them was how in the name of hell Gunnar had ended up at the fire scene. Had he snuck onto the engine. Had he come with one of the ambulances. Had he asked to come? If so, why? He was far from being a little boy who was in love with fire trucks.

My stomach tightened at the fact I didn't know the answer. I hadn't seen much of Gunnar since he'd started to feel better. My mother had been spending a little time with him, but to be honest, I felt like I was getting a little too close for comfort.

In actuality, I hadn't been close enough to him. Physically, anyway. I could handle a relationship that was pure sex. Good hard fucking followed by each of us sleeping in our own bed was right up my alley. This getting to know you bullshit, and him getting to know me, was as foreign as sprouting wings and being able to fly.

I pulled into the parking lot for the Emergency Room and saw both Firehouse Three ambulances in the bay. They must not have gotten here that much sooner than we did. I turned to Gunnar, who hadn't said a word since we'd gotten in the car. "How are you holding up?"

Gunnar startled, yelping as he pulled back from me. It took a few seconds for a look of recognition to dawn in his eyes. "I'm fine. Just worried about Ozzy and Dillon."

The grieving husband and father had been so distraught, he'd been threatening to kill himself. The second ambulance had sedated him and was bringing him to Gloucester Mercy as well. "I think they'll both be okay. Ozzy will be back on his feet tomorrow morning and Dillon will survive this. It will take a long time, but he'll get through it.

Gunnar nodded and went to unbuckle his seatbelt. It wouldn't unhook. No matter how hard he yanked and pulled, the buckle wouldn't release.

Not wanting to startle him again, I set a hand on his shoulder. "Let me help you." My eyes stayed locked on his as I moved both hands to the seatbelt. Some awful instinct in me told me to lean in for a kiss. I fought it tooth and nail. Gunnar was fucked in the head after what he'd seen tonight. I'd be King Douchebag if I took advantage of him in this state. My finger found the release button for the belt. I pushed it and the buckle popped free.

"Thanks." Gunnar was panting. Possibly because I'd been about to kiss him, but more likely because he'd started to panic over being trapped in his seat.

The humidity hit me like a hammer. I couldn't believe it was still this warm at half past midnight. The cop in me couldn't help thinking this heatwave was only urging the arsonist to accelerate his original game plan. He'd started out only setting fires in abandoned buildings and now he was targeting residential neighborhoods and families.

I set a hand on Gunnar's shoulder. Thankfully, he didn't startle this time. "Tell me what you're thinking. Maybe I can help."

Gunnar turned to me. His green eyes were glittering under the fluorescent lights of the parking lot. "Those little girls." A lone tear slid down his cheek. "They never had a chance. Why couldn't the mother get them out of the house?"

I'd been wondering the same thing. "I don't think we'll be able to answer that until we talk to Ozzy, Chasten, and Dillon. The father will know where everyone was in the house and Ozzy might know why the mother stayed put upstairs instead of trying to escape."

"Why couldn't the ladder get there in time?" Tears were streaking down Gunnar's face. "If it had moved faster, the guys would have been able to swing it over to the house and save everyone."

I didn't want to say it out loud, but I'd been wondering the same thing. "I think the 911 call is going to unlock a big part of this mystery."

"What do you mean?" Gunnar swiped the back of his hand over his eyes. He was regaining control of himself.

"You saw where that house was." I knew Gunnar was in no state to play detective, but I needed him to understand what had happened.

"Yeah, out in the middle of nowhere."

"Dillon was on the first floor and the mother and kids were upstairs. What does that say to you?" I kept a close eye on Gunnar's reaction.

Gunnar's face went from confused to eureka in half a second. "That house was in the boondocks. The mom and the kids were upstairs sleeping, and Dillon was downstairs. Maybe he'd fallen asleep watching television."

"Exactly. The fire didn't wake any of them up." I'd been going over that in my head since Ozzy and Chasten came out of that house carrying the bodies of the McMasters family.

"I didn't hear a smoke detector when we arrived."

That was a piece of the puzzle I didn't have. I'd make sure to mention it to Ozzy. "Okay, so you've got a family sleeping unaware as their house burned. So, I ask again, who called 911?"

"The arsonist." Gunnar's mouth dropped open. "Ozzy said they like to watch the fires they set. If his main goal is to burn the house to the ground, why did he call 911? He'd have to know that would send a flurry of activity out there."

Gunnar made a good point. "There are different types of people who set fires. You've got your firebugs who just want to see the world burn. Then you have people who set fires to collect insurance money. Last, are the people looking for revenge."

"Is that what you think is going on? You think someone targeted this family?" Gunnar wore a shocked expression on his face.

"I'm not sure what we're dealing with. Let's get inside and see what's happening with Ozzy." In my years with the Gloucester Police Department, I'd come across all kinds of motives for committing crimes. Money and revenge were the ones I saw most often. If the McMasters fire was set out of revenge, what on earth could members of that family have done that was so severe it warranted being burned to death in their own home, the one place they should have been safe?

Gunnar lapsed back into silence as we headed into the hospital. I asked for Ozzy at the front desk and the nurse on duty led us back to an exam room where Ozzy was sitting on a gurney wearing a blue hospital gown over his uniform pants. I could smell the acrid odor of smoke clinging to him.

"Well, well, well. Look what the cat dragged in. Late to the party as usual." Ozzy's usual grin was in place.

"Here I am." I rolled my eyes at Gunnar, hoping my playful banter with Ozzy would ease his mind. "Had some loose ends to handle at the scene."

"I see you brought one of them with you." Ozzy seemed to be studying Gunnar. "How are you feeling, Noob? Don't think I didn't see you rush out to grab McMasters before he could get to the bodies of his family."

Gunnar deflated before my eyes. I couldn't pinpoint what the hell Ozzy had said to cause that kind of visceral reaction in him. I took a step closer to Gunnar just in case. I wasn't about to let Ozzy's big fucking mouth hurt this kid any more than he'd already been hurt tonight.

"I'll pack my locker and be out of the firehouse in the morning." Gunnar's head was bent. He seemed to be studying his shoes.

Of all the things Gunnar could have said in that moment, this was the last thing I expected to hear him say. What the fuck had he done at the fire scene that would warrant him losing his job? Unless one of my original suppositions was correct and he had snuck on board the fire truck.

"Pack your things? Gunnar, you saved part of our crime scene. You're a hero."

"A hero?" Gunnar looked up at Ozzy. His face was twisted in a mask of confusion. "Three people died while I watched. All I did was stop a grieving father from getting to his family."

The look on Ozzy's face softened. "I don't know what Kennedy told you on the way over here, but I saw signs in that house that this was another arson, which means that house and the victims of the crime are potential evidence. If McMasters had touched them, he could have contaminated the scene. It's an easy way to throw an arson investigation in a different direction if you're the one who set the fire."

Gunnar's eyes narrowed. "Wait, you think Dillon set the fire that killed his family?"

I'd seen fathers annihilate their families in any number of ways. Not that I was going to tell Gunnar that now. "I don't know." That was the best answer I could give at the moment.

"If he did kill them, then by stopping him from contaminating the scene, you preserved evidence. Same goes if Dillon didn't kill his family." Ozzy cringed. His scar twisted as he grimaced. "On the other hand, if there is evidence on those bodies that will help secure a conviction against the person who set this fire, how much more devastating would it be for Dillon to know he was responsible for losing it?"

I could see Gunnar was taking this all in, trying to see the story from both angles. "None of this is easy."

"I had my eyes on you as much as I could, given the situation," Ozzy started with a careful tone in his voice. He shot me a knowing look. "There were several times where you wanted to run into that burning building. Don't try to deny it. I saw it in your eyes."

Instead of replying, Gunnar grabbed a plastic chair and sunk wearily into it.

"On the way to the hospital, Hal told me what the two of you talked about earlier today." Ozzy's serious tone was setting off warning bells in my head. What had Gunnar and Hal been talking about today.

"What's this?" Shit, my voice sounded edgy and tinged with jealousy. I was such an asshole. Here Gunnar was, trying to process the worst thing he'd ever witnessed, and I was acting like a prick because a man I had no claim to was speaking to someone else. Way to go, assclown.

Ozzy shot me a pointed look. He was no dummy. My brother knew exactly where I was coming from. "Hal said you were curious about how people decided to run into danger when everyone else was running away."

"Yeah," Gunnar nodded. "I wanted to know if it was something you were born with or something that came out at the right time."

Christ, that's what Gunnar and Hal had been talking about? I really was a prick. Why had Gunnar asked Hal instead of me? That was an easy question to answer. It probably had to do with the fact that I'd barely seen Gunnar in a week.

"I think tonight answered that question. Don't you?" There was no snark in Ozzy's voice.

This was one of the things I loved best about my brother. He had this innate ability to teach by leading you to the answer instead of handing it to you.

"All I wanted to do was help that family. They were complete strangers to me, and I just wanted to run in there and save those babies." Gunnar took a shaky breath.

I set a hand on his shoulder, letting him know I was there for him without being too pushy.

"Ozzy's right. I did answer my own question." The look on Gunnar's face blossomed into pure wonder. "This was inside me all along." He looked at his hands as if they were magical. "I guess it was just waiting for the right moment to make an appearance."

"I knew it all along," Ozzy said, like a proud papa. "I want to sit down and talk some things over with you. My office, tomorrow at two. Don't be late." Ozzy pointed a finger at Gunnar.

"Captain Graves," a handsome ER doc was standing in the door with his shoulder against the jamb. He wore an annoyed look on his face, like this wasn't his first rodeo with Ozzy. "Reschedule the meeting, you're not going anywhere."

"Is that so, Doc?" Ozzy drew himself up to his full height. His chest puffed out and he looked like he was ready to take a swing at the doctor.

"Stark Givens." The doc held out his hand to shake with Gunnar. "Maybe you can talk some sense into your boss's fool head. Lord knows I've never been able to." The doc was shaking Gunnar's hand, but hadn't taken his eyes off Ozzy.

Stark and Ozzy went way back. He'd chosen Gloucester Mercy for his residency and never left. The good doctor had been treating our bumps, bruises, and other injuries for nearly ten years. I'd always thought there was something a bit deeper going on between the two of them and the grudging smile on my brother's face did nothing to change my mind.

"Gunnar Prince," he returned. "I'm no doctor," Gunnar said pulling his hand free, "but I'm guessing that burn is at least second degree."

"Oh, and where did you go to medical school?" Stark turned a brilliant smile on Gunnar.

Gunnar returned it with one of his own. It made my heart thud in my chest to see that smile flashed at another man. "I watch a lot of *Greys* and *ER*. Looks second degree to me."

That smile appeared again, but this time, there was something different about it. I thought it was almost predatory.

"Lay off, Stark." Ozzy wore a no-nonsense look. "Tomorrow at two, kid. Get a good night's sleep. Take him home, Kennedy."

I saw the look of disappointment on Stark's face as I led Gunnar out of the room. It was obvious I had a decision to make. Did I go for it with Gunnar and see if he was interested in me as more than a lover, or did I drop him off and walk away?

As we headed toward the parking lot, I honestly had no idea which direction to take.

20

Gunnar

I didn't know if it was leftover adrenaline from what happened tonight or the possessive way Kennedy grabbed my hand and practically pulled me out of the room after that ER doc nearly drooled over me, but I was amped up.

Thank Christ it was dark because my dick was so hard and heavy, I was sure it could be seen from space.

Kennedy seemed to be in a weird mood as well. I'd never seen him act possessive over me. I couldn't tell if it had to do with him thinking Doctor McHotpants was a bad move for me or if he was acting this way because he wanted me for himself. I wasn't a mind reader. If he wanted me, he was going to have to tell me.

Stark Givens had absolutely no trouble telegraphing exactly what he wanted. That man was going to fuck me until I drained him dry. I might be young and a bit inexperienced, but I knew the look of a man who desperately wanted to lose himself in me.

Kennedy, on the other hand, was giving me the impression he was just hanging around to save me from myself, like some kind of guardian angel. He was always turning up when I needed him, but aside from that one night on his balcony after he'd had a bit to drink, he'd never made another move on me.

What was worse, a man who was obvious in his desire for a one-night stand, or a man who was a complete fucking enigma? At this moment in time, I was going with enigma.

Kennedy parked the SUV in his driveway and before I could say anything, he was out of the car and heading toward my door. I guessed we were adding chivalrous to Kennedy's list of traits.

When he opened the door, I was quick to hop out, but Kennedy's strong right arm stopped me. I bumped back against the side panel of the SUV. There was a dangerous look in his blue eyes, which looked black in the dim light of the quarter moon.

"Strip," Kennedy commanded. There was no hint of a smile in his eyes. He looked dead serious.

"Strip? What the hell is wrong with you, caveman? It might be the middle of the night, but we've got neighbors, you know? I'm not going to let you take me against your patrol vehicle like I'm some kind of fucking rent boy."

"Rent boy?" Kennedy moved closer to me. The hard plane of his chest bumped against me, pinning me against the window. "That's exactly how Stark Givens would have treated you. He would have used you up and kicked you out."

"Who says I wasn't in the mood to be used." I wasn't, but that was beside the point.

Kennedy's eyes flashed. "Wrong answer."

Wrong answer? What the hell was he talking about?

Before I knew what was happening, Kennedy was ripping my shirt over my head. I heard seams pop as he muscled it over my shoulders. He threw it to the ground to land in a puddle on the driveway. "What is wrong with you?" My voice echoed into the night.

Not bothering to answer me, Kennedy went for the button on my jeans. I was still hard as a rock. It wasn't going to take much to set me off. Kennedy's rough hands on my hips yanking the denim downward brought my attention back to him. He was down on his knees, eye level with my bulge and it didn't seem to phase him. Not one bit. In fact, it seemed to be making him angrier. Who the hell got pissed off at an erection they caused?

My pants hit the tops of my shoes. I could feel the humid air against my bare skin. The hungry look in Kennedy's eyes was going to be the death of me. I couldn't figure out if he was going to run his hand over my cock or lick it through the cotton fabric of my jockey shorts.

Kennedy did neither. He stood up slowly. His entire body sliding against mine. His dick was as hot and hard as my own. The only difference was that it felt like a monster. I had a feeling he knew exactly how to wield it.

His hands dropped back down to my hips. His dick jumped against my stomach. I was ready for this. So fucking ready. His hands dug into my skin. Any second now, he was going to rip my underwear down and go for it right here in the driveway.

I wasn't prepared for him to spin me around, flattening me against the side panel of the SUV. My face was pressed against the cool glass, while my torso was flush with the passenger back door. "What the fuck, Kennedy?" I managed to grunt.

Kennedy pressed himself against me. I could feel the heat of him melting into my back. He felt like he was on fire. "What the fuck?" I felt his lips curl into a smile against the back of my ear. "I asked you to do something and you didn't do it. Every time I ask you to do something you go and do just the opposite."

"You're not my keeper, Kennedy." I wanted him to be. Badly. Whatever the hell was going on here had my entire body on edge. I'd never been so completely aroused by someone before. I'd had a few random blow jobs over the years, but that only involved my dick and some stranger's mouth. This was different. It was like Kennedy had somehow known where my switch was. His touch lit up my entire body. I pressed my ass back against him. His dick twitched against me.

"That's right, Gunnar. I'm *not* your keeper. If I was, you would obey me. You wouldn't let a man-whore like Stark Givens fuck you with his eyes right in front of me."

Fuck me with his eyes? I'd never heard it put like that before, but I had to admit Kennedy had a point. "How am I supposed to stop something like that from happening? Christ, I'm twenty-one years old. My dick gets hard when the wind changes direction."

Kennedy growled against the back of my neck. His right hand slid down my side and across to my dick. He gave it a squeeze. I moaned out loud, bucking into his touch. His hand lit a fire in me I wasn't going to be able to put out on my own. "Is that what *this* is? A stiff breeze did this to your dick? I don't fucking think so? This is all me, get it? All me, Gunnar."

"All you," I whispered. My own voice was nearly unrecognizable.

"That's a good boy." Kennedy gave my package one last squeeze before pulling his hand back. "Good, but not good enough." A loud smack rang out.

What the hell? Did Kennedy just fucking spank me? For the first time in my life, I was absolutely speechless. I didn't know if I should tell him to stop or ask for another. Christ, my body was a mess of sensations I wasn't quite sure how to interpret.

"At least I've got your attention." There was a menacing tone to Kennedy's voice. It sounded dark and most definitely aroused.

Oh, yeah. Kennedy was getting off on this. The bigger question was what I felt. Was I getting off on this too or was some other emotion trying to work its way to the surface? I didn't have much time to ponder that question. Another swat landed against my ass. It was harder than the first one. Thankfully, my underwear provided my cheeks some protection from his strong hand.

"This doesn't seem to be getting much of a reaction out of you, boy. Is it because you know you're bad and think you deserve to be punished?"

Christ, was that it? Did I want him to give it to me for being such a jerk to him on the day we met? Or maybe for flirting with Hal at Sunday dinner? Or letting the good doctor eye me like I was a prime cut of meat? "Yes," I managed to whisper.

"That's a good boy." Kennedy slid his hand down my back. One finger slid beneath the waistband.

I thought the sweet torture of that move alone was going to kill me. "Kennedy," I pled.

"That's right. You know you want this." His finger slid the length of my crack, pulling my briefs down with it. The sultry night air against my bare skin only made me hotter.

Using his other hand, Kennedy pulled my underwear down past the swell of my ass. "Gorgeous." His hands caressed my naked skin. Puffs of his hot breath blew against the back of my neck. This little passion play was just as arousing to him as it was to me.

"Now, you're going to be my good boy and take this, aren't you? We wouldn't want the neighbors to hear you, now would we?"

All I could do was shake my head no.

Kennedy's first swat against my bare ass made my dick jump in a way I didn't know was possible. It stung like hell and I was sure there was a perfect imprint of his hand against my skin, but somehow it ratcheted up my need for him. A breathy moan escaped me.

"You liked that, didn't you?" Not giving me time to answer, Kennedy swatted my other cheek. He was the one to moan this time when his jean-clad dick brushed against my ass.

"Kennedy…" I begged. I was on the edge. One more whack and I was going to lose control all over the passenger door.

"You're so close, aren't you? Close enough you can taste it." Kennedy's words vibrated against the shell of my ear. His low voice brought me right up to the edge. What the hell was happening to me? It was as if Kennedy knew just how to play my body. As if he were the only man who could make me feel controlled, yet free. Untouched, but precariously balanced.

The next swat landed firmly against my left cheek. The slap of skin on skin echoed through the sleeping neighborhood. "Come for me, boy!"

All it took was his raspy voice in my ear and I was gone. My dick throbbed. My breath stuck in my throat. When my release hit, I felt like I was being sucked into the eye of a hurricane. I could feel Kennedy's body pressed to mine. He was everywhere. My dick pumped spurt after spurt of cream in tune with my pounding heart. I cried out for Kennedy, forgetting his rule that I be still. One large hand clamped down over my lips.

Kennedy was rocking himself back and forth against my bare ass. He was using me to get himself off. For whatever reason, that made me come so much harder. He groaned against the back of my neck and I felt a warm spot growing against my ass. He'd come too.

With a strangled half moan, Kennedy backed away from me. I wasn't sure I had the strength to keep myself upright. I could only imagine what I looked like, angry red handprints on both cheeks of my ass, my jizz splattered against the side of the SUV, my face was so hot, I'm sure I looked like a boiled lobster.

"Fucking A!" Kennedy panted. "Clean that up and go to bed." With that final order, he turned and walked away from me.

I turned to watch him go. There was something different about the way he was walking. Usually, he stood to his full height, towering over nearly everyone he met. His stride was confident with a bit of his natural cockiness thrown in. As he walked away now, his posture was slumped. I couldn't figure out if it was in ecstasy or in defeat.

21

"I fucking came in my pants like a horny teenager." I slapped my hand on the bar, not wanting to look at Hennessey's face.

Hennessey was the most level-headed of all my brothers. Ozzy was a hothead. Dallas acted before he thought things through, but I could always count on Hen to stay the course and hear me out. I'd told him everything that happened last night from the call to the McMasters' fire scene, to what happened at the hospital with Stark Givens, and ending with Gunnar and I both coming like wildfire, cocks untouched.

When I finally got the courage to look my brother in the eye, Hennessey was holding a damp towel. Before I'd finished speaking, he'd been polishing the bar with it. There was an unreadable look in his icy blue eyes. I knew he'd speak when he had his thoughts in order, but Christ, I was dying here.

"Sounds to me like you both got what you needed, even though neither of you knew you needed it." He set the cloth on the bar and grabbed two bottles of water. He handed one to me before drinking half of his in one swallow. Small drops of water clung to the lower bristles of his moustache.

I opened my mouth to tell him he was so fucking wrong, but then it hit me. Maybe my brother was right.

"It's been years since Micah fucked you over. Hell, I can't remember the last time you went on a date. I can't even remember the last time someone besides you touched your dick." Hen scratched the side of his beard, his eyes twinkling at me as if he were challenging me to prove him wrong.

My stomach clenched at the mention of my ex's name. Micah Hills had been my rookie ride-along partner during his probationary period with the Gloucester Police Department. He'd been into me from the moment we met and stupidly, I'd encouraged his behavior. It was against the rules for us to fraternize since I was his superior officer. That should have mattered, but it didn't. We burned so hot and bright together that a flame out was inevitable. When that happened and he'd moved on to his next lover, I was devastated. Stupidly, I'd fallen in love with the kid and he'd broken my heart so badly that I never wanted to fall in love again. "What if this is Micah all over again?" That had been my biggest fear all along. It was the reason why I'd kept trying to keep Gunnar at arm's distance since we met.

Hennessey sighed. "Are you a psychic? No! So there's no way of knowing." He sounded matter of fact, which was what I needed. Hen's straightforwardness was the reason I'd come to him instead of Ozzy or Dallas.

"That doesn't help much," I groaned.

"Here's what we know. From what Mom and Dad say, he's a good kid, err, guy. He's not out to take advantage of you and they said he was truly grateful for the help. Ozzy loves him too. Says he's the best noob he's ever had. Said Gunnar does everything he's asked without complaint." Hennessey shrugged his broad shoulders. "If you ask me, those are two ringing endorsements right there, but the final decision is yours. Do you want to risk your heart again?"

My brother made several good points. I hadn't thought about what our parents and Ozzy thought of him. I could only imagine that after what happened last night at the fire scene, with Gunnar helping to keep Dillon McMasters from tampering with the scene, that Ozzy would be even more over the moon about Gunnar. If I were honest with myself, I'd also have to admit I hadn't seen any red warning flags about the kid. *Yet*, my traitorous brain supplied.

I pushed that last thought aside. "I think I could be."

"Take him out on a date. A *real* date. Pay for dinner. See a movie. Kiss him on his doorstep. Go home alone. Jack off." Hen waggled his bushy blond brows at me.

"Micah and I never really dated," I said absently. We fucked like bunnies and called out for pizza. Come to think of it, we ate a lot of fucking pizza during that time. We never cooked for each other or really talked. All we did was have sex.

"I remember that," Hennessey said quietly. "We all knew he was bad news, but you wouldn't listen."

I could see the sadness in my brother's eyes. It was clear how much Hen loved me. I'd been so angry at him when he and the others told me Micah was no good. We'd almost come to blows over it. When things ended with him getting a job with the Boston Police Department, not only did I lose the man I thought I was in love with, but I'd had some bridge-mending to do with my brothers. None of them made it easy. Those were some dark-ass days. "What if it happens again?"

Hen sighed. He reached over the bar to give my shoulders a shake. "One day at a time, man. One day at a time."

It was odd that my brother was quoting the AA motto to me in the middle of his bar. "Thanks, Dr. Phil." I snorted, and before long we were laughing like loons.

"No one knows what tomorrow is going to bring. Be happy in this moment, but keep your eyes open all the same."

Hennessey wasn't wrong. Get lost in the moment, but not so lost that you can't see the forest for the trees. "This is why I came to see you, man."

"I know. Ozzy would have told you to fuck Gunnar until your dick fell off and Dallas would have told you to walk away now while you still had a chance."

Again, my brother hit the nail on the head. I wasn't the only one in the family who'd nursed a broken heart or two over the last few years. My mother had convinced herself she was never going to be a Mimi. My father had gotten her a rescue kitten from the shelter across town hoping it would help. She might not openly talk about grandchildren anymore, but I knew she was still thinking about them. "Thanks, Hennessey. How about some hot wings before I have to leave for work?"

"Are you sure? How are you supposed to pick up hookers if your car smells like Buffalo wings and stale ass?" His moustache twitched and he started to laugh.

"Fine, I'll have a cheeseburger." When Hen was right. He was right.

About everything. While he went to give my order to the kitchen, I pulled out my phone and sent a text to Gunnar.

22

Gunnar

Date night? It was more like faint night. Christ, Kennedy was going to be here any minute now and I was a fucking wreck. I'd already changed my shirt three times and I still didn't think I looked good enough for him.

What the hell kind of game was he playing asking me out on a date anyway? At least I knew where I stood when he was barking out orders and grinding his cock against my ass. Now, I had no fucking clue what to do.

Ozzy had told me to just act natural, but he'd said it with his trademark shit-eating grin on his face. I had no idea if he was serious or seriously fucking with me.

Making matters worse was the fact that Kennedy wouldn't tell me anything about our plans. I didn't know if we were going to a real restaurant to eat or down to the beach for a picnic. Not that I would be able to eat anyway. My stomach was tossing and turning so hard I was feeling seasick.

At 7:00 p.m., on the button, my doorbell rang. Before I opened the door, I took one last deep breath to settle myself down. I didn't want to jump on Kennedy and ruin our night before it got started.

Kennedy was standing on my doorstep in dress pants and a jacket. It was ninety-one degrees out and he was dressed to the nines. Hell, I was wearing the only pair of jeans I owned without an artful rip in the knee and a tropical shirt with turtles and palm trees.

We hadn't seemed so different the other night when we were getting off against Kennedy's SUV, but in the stark light of day, we were miles apart. "Uh, hi," I managed to stammer. He looked good enough to eat.

"These are for you." Kennedy handed me a small bouquet of coral-colored Gerbera daisies. They were spectacular.

My breath caught in my throat as I looked back and forth between Kennedy and the flowers. "Come in." I ushered him inside and moved toward the kitchen. I'd thought it odd when I'd found a small glass vase under my sink when I went looking for a new scrub brush for the dishes. I figured it had been another little gift from David and Mandy. It would come in handy now.

I could feel Kennedy watching me as I busied myself with the flowers. When I was finished, I set them in the center of the dining table. No one had ever gotten me flowers before. I wasn't sure what I should do at this point. "They're gorgeous. Thank you so much. I don't have anything for you."

Kennedy laughed and held his hand out for me. "Yes, you do. You're going to tell me all about yourself over dinner. Do you like seafood?"

"I do." I couldn't believe this was happening to me. I was going out on a date with the best-looking man I'd ever met in my life.

"Good. I know the perfect place down by the harbor."

I'd take Kennedy's word for that. Even though I'd grown up in Rockport, which was one town over from Gloucester, I didn't know my new home that well. It was just a place I drove through on the highway to get away from my parents. Gloucester was beginning to feel more like home every day.

Kennedy escorted me out to his truck, which I'd never seen before. It was this hulking black Ford that I needed to use the running boards to climb up into. "Where have you been hiding this beast?"

He grinned at me as he hooked his seatbelt. "I keep it in the garage. I mostly use the police SUV. So long as I'm on my way to work or on my way home, it's okay to pick up a pizza or a bag or two of groceries. It's been awhile since I took her out for a spin." Kennedy lovingly caressed the door.

The truck was top of the line. Leather seats. Full navigation system. I'd seen the tow hitch and the snowplow hook up. I could see Kennedy plowing out his neighbors' driveway during snowstorms.

While Kennedy drove, I made sure to notice where he was turning. It was high time I got to know more about this town than how to drive to the fire station and back home again. I could smell the ocean as we drove toward the harbor. The ocean always comforted me.

"This is it." Kennedy pulled into a parking lot of a place called The Blue Collar Lobster Company.

I looked at the restaurant which sat right on the harbor. There were fishing boats in the marina behind it. The sign featured a blue lobster coming out of a pot. This was exactly the kind of place I pictured Kennedy taking us to. There were a lot of expensive places to eat seafood in this corner of Massachusetts, but The Blue Collar Lobster Company looked perfect for a couple of blue collar guys like us.

While I'd been thinking about how perfect this place was, Kennedy had walked over to my door. He opened it for me and held a hand out to help me down. God help me, but I felt like a princess being helped down from her carriage by her romantic prince.

"I hope you don't mind, but I made reservations."

"Why would I mind?" Kennedy was blowing me away with his gentlemanly behavior. Much more of this being catered to and I was going to find myself in some serious trouble with Kennedy Lynch.

Kennedy shrugged my question off as he opened the door to the restaurant. There was something he wasn't telling me. Something that was close to the surface. I wanted to ask about it but didn't want to ruin our night all the same. I kept my mouth shut as he checked us in at the hostess stand and she waved us into the restaurant.

What caught my eye instantly about the dining room was the wall of windows facing the harbor. I could see more fishing vessels and the Cape Pond Ice building a bit further out. Past that was a lighthouse. The red light in the tower seemed to be flashing every ten seconds or so. Gloucester Harbor was incredible.

The place was packed. There were families in the lobby waiting to be seated and nearly every table in the place was filled. More tables were outside on the open-air deck. I assumed the open tables were for people who'd made reservations like Kennedy. When we got to the table, there was another surprise waiting for me. Not only was there a sign with our names on it, wishing us a happy first date, but there was a box sitting on my bread plate. It was wrapped in silver glitter paper.

The box wasn't the only thing glittering. So was Kennedy's smile. He looked absolutely dazzling. Before we'd gotten into the truck, he'd shed the suit jacket and had rolled his sleeves up to his elbows. My man was magnificent.

The tables were dressed in a red and white checkerboard pattern with small hurricane lamps burning. It gave the restaurant a soft glow which was magnified by the reflection of lamps in the bank of windows. "Wow! This place is amazing."

Kennedy was all smiles. "I thought you'd enjoy getting to see the harbor."

"After we eat, can we go out on the deck? I want to get a better look at the lighthouse." I was hoping we'd take a selfie or two with the harbor behind us.

"Sure. That's Ten Pound Island you're looking at out there. It got its name because ten pounds is what the English settlers paid the local Indian tribe for the land."

"You're a fount of knowledge." I couldn't help smiling at Kennedy.

Instead of returning my grin, Kennedy's face grew serious. "When I landed with David and Mandy, they told me they were my parents and Gloucester was my home. I'd only been with them for a few weeks when they started the paperwork to officially adopt me." Kennedy's eyes had gone glassy. "I decided that since I was going to live here, I wanted to know everything about the city. We went on weekend adventures to all kinds of places here in town. Week by week, I got to know my new hometown as well as my brothers and parents. Mandy told me once that those weekends at Good Harbor Beach or kayaking out to the Ten Pound Lighthouse were the best memories of her life."

I nodded along with the story. I had nothing to compare that to. "We never took vacations. My father was so obsessed with running the first dealership, and then the second, that he never dared to take any time off at all." Christ, I sounded like a sad sack.

"This is where you start." Kennedy pointed out the window. "For whatever reason, you landed here. Make the most of it."

Kennedy was right. When I took my eyes off the harbor to look at him, he was buried in his menu. I hadn't given a thought to eating. I'd been so lost in his eyes that the scents of the fresh-boiled lobster and steamed clams hadn't penetrated my consciousness.

Following his lead, I picked up my menu. As much as I loved lobster, the last thing I wanted to do was deal with trying to crack one open on a first date. Lobsters were a messy business and by the time you were finished eating one, your hands smelled like the crustacean for hours afterward. Not exactly a prelude to romance when you had fish fingers.

"I'm thinking of double baked-stuffed lobster. What about you?" Kennedy's blue eyes shone over the top of his menu.

Actually, baked-stuffed wasn't a bad idea. The tail meat was chopped and then tossed with scallops and a Ritz cracker stuffing and baked in the shell. All I'd need to crack open and eat would be the claws. I could live with that. "Same," I agreed. "With an order of fried calamari to start?" I waggled my eyebrows at him.

Kennedy laughed. "Anything you want. This night is all about you."

"Why?" I asked without thinking. It didn't make me want the answer any less.

"Because I've been such a jerk." He laughed at himself. "From the day we met I've been nothing but rude to you. Then after that with pushing you away, pulling you close, barking out orders like I was some kind of billionaire Dom from a movie. This is my way of asking you to start over. Start fresh."

It was my turn to laugh. Kennedy was a lot of things, but he was no Christian Grey. "We both got off to a rocky start with each other, but that didn't stop you from always being there for me when I needed you. Even when I didn't realize I needed you, there you were. Like at the fire the other night. You were my guardian angel."

Kennedy opened his mouth but was interrupted by the waitress. He ordered for both of us, getting us both sodas to drink instead of beer. I liked that. He was serious enough about me and this date to be sober for it all.

When the waitress left, he was back to grinning at me. "Are you going to open your present?"

My eyes slid back to the glittery box sitting near my right hand. "How did you do this? Get this to be on my plate?"

"It's a service the restaurant provides. I could have ordered flowers too, but since I was bringing some to your door, I figured this was the perfect gift."

So far as I was concerned, this was the perfect date. Whatever was in this box was just the cherry on top of the sundae. I picked up the box, giving it a little shake. Something slid around inside. Not wanting to wait another moment, I tore the paper off. It was a box of chocolates, but not any chocolates, they were shaped like lobsters. "Kennedy! This is amazing." I could feel my emotions starting to creep up. If I wasn't careful, I was going to end up blubbering at the table.

"Here are your drinks, guys." The waitress set down two Cokes with paper straws.

"To you, Gunnar." Kennedy held his glass up. "No matter what life has thrown at you these last few weeks, you've been up to the challenge."

I touched our glasses together. They pinged in unison. My heart was hammering so hard, I could barely hear myself think. "I've been able to go with the flow because of you."

Kennedy opened his mouth to say something when the waitress came back with the calamari.

I was anxious to dive in. My appetite had returned with Kennedy's kindness, but now I could see there was something on his mind. "What is it?"

"I've tried to say this twice now and both times I've been interrupted. I'm just going to say it now in case the waitress comes back to ask us how everything tastes."

Now I was nervous. Kennedy seemed amped up and his eyes were unreadable. Was he going to tell me the date was fun, but it couldn't go beyond this? Christ, I was a wreck. "I'm listening."

"I want to give this thing between us a chance," he blurted out, looking shocked at himself.

I couldn't breathe. Did Kennedy just say what I think he said or was I having a stroke?

"Gunnar? Are you okay?" Kennedy's smile had faded to a look of concern.

"Yes!" I gushed, nearly knocking over my water glass.

"Yes, you're okay or yes, you want to see where this thing between us goes?"

"Both." I was stunned. I was sitting at a table, in a perfect restaurant, with a gorgeous man who wanted to date me. I didn't know how this had become my life, but I wasn't going to take one second of it for granted.

23

Kennedy

The food at The Blue Collar Lobster was out of this world. Hennessey had been the one to tell me about the restaurant. He'd taken a date or two there because it was just down the street from the bar. None of his dates had appreciated that fact.

Gunnar's eyes hadn't stopped twinkling from the time I picked him up. He'd had as good a time as I had. Now came the moment of truth: the goodnight kiss. I still hadn't decided if I was going to take Hennessey's advice and end the night on that kiss or if it was going to lead something else.

We'd both been quiet during the drive back home. It was an easy silence, not one of those fraught with awkwardness. We were comfortable being together. I couldn't help but think if Gunnar was wondering what was going to happen when I pulled the truck into the driveway.

He didn't have long to ponder. My headlights flashed against the garage as I parked the car. My hands were sweating as I pulled the key out of the ignition. Without saying a word, I hopped out of the truck and walked around to Gunnar's side. He clutched his box of chocolates in one hand and took mine with the other.

"I had the best time tonight."

"I did too." Lacing our hands together, I walked him to his front steps. "Good night," I whispered before bending forward to kiss my date. Gunnar was my date. I still couldn't believe it.

When our lips connected it was like coming home. My heart thundered in my chest. It beat harder when Gunnar's hand came up to frame the side of my face. I moaned against his lips, wanting more. I wanted it all.

"Are you sure you want to say good night?" Gunnar's eyes were back to twinkling at me. "I make a mean bowl of Cheerios in the morning."

"Are you asking me to spend the night?" My dick was filling at light speed. I swore I started feeling dizzy.

"I thought I was being very clear. Yes. Spend the night with me."

"How could I resist?" I bent to press a sweet kiss to his lips. Gunnar's hands dug into my hips. He pulled me flush against him. He was as hot and ready for me as I was for him.

Gunnar reluctantly pulled back, fishing his keys out of his pocket. He climbed the stairs and opened the door. He crooked his finger at me, motioning me inside. I hoped I knew what I was doing, that this was the right decision and not some colossal mistake.

I followed him into the house. Gunnar shut and locked the door behind me. He leaned against it with a devious look on his face. "I've got you right where I want you."

Striding toward Gunnar, his look went from mischievous, to turned on, to alarmed in a matter of seconds. I snorted as I scooped him into my arms and carried him like a bride toward the stairs. He wrapped his arms around my neck, resting his face on my shoulder.

"Are you sure this is what you want?" I set Gunnar down on the floor at the foot of his bed. I noticed the bed was made and the room was neat as a pin.

"You are what I want, Kennedy." Gunnar lifted his shirt over his head. It dropped soundlessly to the floor.

My first instinct was to go to him and rip the rest of his clothes off. I took a deep breath and tried to slow myself down. "Now your pants." I had no idea where this take charge instinct came from. I'd never been like this with any other lover, only Gunnar. Was it because I was so much older than him or because this was how it was supposed to be?

Gunnar's slender hands went to the waistband of his pants. His fingers deftly undid the top button of his jeans. They drew down the zipper, while he shot me a devilish smile.

My eyes were glued to his hands as they pushed the denim off his ass and down past the sizable bulge in his briefs. I could feel my mouth start to water. Christ, Gunnar was making me feel like a teenager about to go off in my pants for the second time with him.

"Your turn," Gunnar challenged. He was standing there in his navy briefs, the head of his cock pushing up past the waistband.

I was about to do what Gunnar asked when I paused with my shirt halfway up my stomach. My entire body felt as if it were on fire. Getting my clothes off was the first step, but I wanted help. "You do it."

Gunnar's eyes glowed brighter at the thought of being able to strip me bare. He stalked toward me like a panther. He didn't stop in front of me to get right to it, instead, he stepped behind me. I could feel the heat of him sinking into my back. One finger slipped beneath the hem of my shirt. It burned a trail along my waistline as Gunnar moved to the front of me. His hands slid beneath my shirt, rubbing slowly over my abs. It was sweet torture. "Are you going to pet me like a cat or take my clothes off."

"We're only going to have one first time together." There was a look of wonder in his eyes. Who was I to disappoint him?

I flinched every time his skin touched mine as he worked my shirt up and over my head. More than anything, I wanted to push him on the bed and have my way with him. It was taking every last shred of self-control to stay put.

A blast of cold air hit my skin when Gunnar finally got my shirt off. Both of his hands landed on my back, exploring every inch of skin. "You're perfection," he whispered, stepping around to the front of me. Those same hands slid down my chest to tangle in the fur over my stomach.

"Hardly," I scoffed.

"I guess we'll just have to agree to disagree." Gunnar sank to his knees. This position reminded me so much of the night he tried to thank me for helping him out.

I reached down, caressing his face with my right hand. "Hurry," I whispered. We had all night, but I didn't want to spend all of it involved in this dance.

Gunnar made quick work of my shoes and pants. All that was left were my black boxer briefs with a giant bulge. "I did this to you."

"Christ, you have no idea what you do to me."

He licked his lips before licking over my package. I hissed in response. Even with my boxers on, I could feel the wet heat of his mouth. Slipping my fingers into the waistband, I slid them down just far enough for my long-suffering erection to spring free.

"I need to taste you." Gunnar took a step forward, still on his knees. "Please."

Reaching for his head, I pulled Gunnar's face closer to me. I took myself in hand, rubbing the head of my dick against his silky lips. "Fuck, yeah."

Without being asked, Gunnar opened his mouth. I slipped myself inside. His tongue began to lick and suck me as if this was what he'd been born to do. "That's it. Take all of me." I pushed in slowly until I hit the back of his throat. Gunnar gagged around his mouthful. I couldn't help smiling.

The combination of his eyes glittering up at me and the quiet way he was gagging on my dick had me on the edge in no time. If I didn't pull back, the party was going to end before it began. "Easy. Easy," I panted. Christ, this kid was going to be the death of me.

A look of disappointment graced Gunnar's face.

"Strip and get on the bed." I needed a few seconds to get myself together again. This night wasn't supposed to be all about me. It was about Gunnar too. About us.

After a few deep breaths, I turned around to see Gunnar lying on the center of his bed. His dick was aimed at the ceiling. His hands pillowed behind his head. I knew they were in that position so he wouldn't be tempted to bring himself off. He was on the edge, even though I hadn't touched him yet. "Look at you. So handsome. All mine."

His eyelashes fluttered at me, but he stayed silent.

Kneeling between his spread legs, I could see how nervous he was. I set a hand on his knee, which I slid down lower and lower until my fingers wrapped around his shaft and started stroking. Gunnar practically shot off the bed. I snickered at him as he fell slowly back to the mattress.

"Kennedy, please. I need more."

"Oh, you're going to get more." I lowered my mouth to him, licking slowly around the crown before slipping my lips down over him. Gunnar bucked forward, sending his dick into the back of my throat. I wasn't ready for him to cut off my air like that. I set both hands on his thighs and gently pulled back. "Supplies?" I wasn't going any further than this if Gunnar didn't have condoms and lube.

"Top drawer." He waved a hand in the direction of the nightstand.

The box of condoms was unopened and the plastic wrap on the bottle of lube was still intact. It was obvious Gunnar hadn't been with anyone else since he'd moved into the townhouse. I hadn't been either for that matter. "Are you sure?" I needed to ask him one more time just in case. He was so nervous. I needed to know it was because he was excited about what was going to happen rather than afraid of it.

"Never been more sure about anything in my life. Now hurry up and fuck me!"

I guess that settled that. I suited myself up as quickly as I could, careful to go slow when I lubed my cock. The last thing I needed was to go off in the condom, but outside of Gunnar.

Swiping a lubed finger against Gunnar's hole, I paused for a few seconds to tease him and wriggled my way inside. He was so fucking tight. He clamped down around me. "You're an eager little thing."

"Now, Kennedy, please. I can't wait much longer."

I knew exactly what he was talking about. I couldn't wait any longer either. I finished loosening him up as fast as I could, although, truth be told, I would have loved to tease and torment him this way for much longer. Another time. I shivered at the thought of doing this again.

After adding a bit more lube to my rock-hard dick, I lined myself up with Gunnar's hole. "This is it."

"Do it!" Gunnar urged behind gritted teeth. His green eyes were locked with mine.

"Your wish is my command." I pushed forward, breaching the first ring of muscle. I nearly came then and there. This feeling of euphoria washed over me. I'd never felt anything like that with another man.

"What's wrong?"

I wasn't about to tell him what I was feeling. The last thing I needed was for Gunnar to see me as a needy guy. One time in the sack didn't make us soulmates. "Nothing, I'm fine." To prove my point, I pushed forward, sending my dick deeper and deeper inside Gunnar. If I were a more whimsical man, I'd swear our souls were touching.

Gunnar's eyes glazed over when I bottomed out. He was trying with all his might to keep himself from coming. At least we were in the same boat.

My instincts were telling me to go hard and fast. I kept them in check by reminding myself I needed to make sure Gunnar was taken care of before my own needs were satisfied.

"Jesus, Kennedy, now." Gunnar was fidgeting beneath me.

All of my good intentions flew out the window. I pulled my hips back as slow as I possibly could before setting a punishing pace. Gunnar cried out my name as his fingers dug into my biceps. There were going to be bruises there in the morning. I couldn't have cared less. I wanted his brand on me for the world to see.

The slap of flesh on flesh filled the room. I was mesmerized by the look I was putting on Gunnar's face. It was somewhere between ecstasy and agony. I couldn't help but wonder if I was wearing a similar look.

"Close," Gunnar panted.

"Me too." I'd been thinking about my high school gym teacher to keep from coming. She'd been under five feet tall and fond of over-using her whistle. I slipped my hand around Gunnar's cock, jacking him in time to the beat of my hips.

"Kennedy!" Gunnar shouted.

Come ripped from his slit to coat my hand. Gunnar's eyes were rolled back in his head. I took a second to freeze-frame that moment in my mind before I let myself go. My dick jerked once. The pleasure was nearly blinding. Just when I thought I was winding down, Gunnar tightened himself around me and I felt like I was coming all over again.

When it was over, my dick ached from the exertion as I slipped from Gunnar's body and removed the condom. I'd taken myself off to the bathroom to clean up. I almost didn't recognize the man in the mirror. He looked happy. He *was* happy.

I had no idea what came next, but I did know that there was a warm man waiting for me to come back to bed. I'd deal with tomorrow, tomorrow.

24

Gunnar

How is it that the best times of your life go by at the speed of light? Those hours with Kennedy last night had been the best I'd ever known. He'd left this morning with a casual, "Catch you later." I had no idea when later was or even if there would actually be a later.

Part of me knew I was being ridiculous. He'd gotten all dressed up last night and made reservations at a restaurant. All for me. What happened in my bed later only brought us closer together. At least that's how I saw it.

After the fireworks, he'd come back to bed with a warm, wet cloth to clean me up before he'd spooned himself around me and fell asleep. I hadn't minded one bit. There were so many things I needed to think about, and I wouldn't have been able to do that if Kennedy had been awake and talking to me.

Granted, he was only the second lover I'd ever had in my life, but I knew from the moment he touched me this thing between us was more. Special. I sounded ridiculous, but I could feel it deep down in my soul.

I didn't have time to think about Kennedy right now. Ozzy had sent a text asking me to meet with him half an hour before my shift began. Thankfully, I was past thinking he was going to fire me, which freed me up to think about the topics he did want to discuss. Chief among them were Kennedy and the McMasters' fire.

It had been days since that fire, but it had stayed with me. The way Dillon cried out for his wife and daughters. Hal and Max covering their bodies with blankets and the way I'd had to hold him back from going to them. I didn't know how the people at the firehouse dealt with these kinds of scenes day in and day out.

Ozzy was sitting at his desk making a funny face at his computer screen when I knocked on his office door.

"Hey, Gunnar. Come in. I can't get this damn report to download." Ozzy rolled his dark eyes.

"Mind if I take a look?"

"Go ahead." Ozzy got out of his seat with a dramatic sigh.

I had a feeling this would be an easy fix but didn't want to sound cocky in front of my new boss. Reading the original email, I hit the button to download the report and instantly was asked for a password. "It's asking for a password."

"I thought I wasn't supposed to give out my password to things I get through the internet." Ozzy wore a confused look on his face.

"That's only for things that are suspect. Like Amazon saying there's a problem with your account and to use a button in the email to log in. Who is this report from?"

"The Gloucester Fire Chief." Ozzy sighed, sounding like all of this shit was beyond him.

"Come over here." I motioned him toward the screen. "When you mouse over the chief's name, his email address pops up in the bottom left-hand corner of the screen. See?" I moused over him name and pointed to the address. "Is that his correct email address?"

"Yeah." Ozzy sounded considerably less cheerful than he had when I knocked on his door.

"Enter your password and the report will pop up. If you get an option to save it, do that so you don't have to go through this again."

"How do you kids keep up with all this shit?" Ozzy pecked in his password with one finger.

To keep you oldsters out of trouble, was my first thought, but I bit my tongue. "I listen to a lot of news." That was the truth. I'd promised myself I'd keep up with local headlines and I was doing just that.

Ozzy's face was a mask of concentration. A moment later, his easy smile was back in place. "Thank you for playing tech support, but that's not why I asked to meet with you."

"Okay." I wasn't sure what the hell else to say, so I shut up. I wasn't about to offer information about something he wasn't going to ask me about. Namely Kennedy.

"I know things got crazy after your ride along." Serious Ozzy was back in charge.

"That's for sure. They were crazy during it too."

"Yes, they were. Scenes like that are par for the course for us. People watching their homes burn never gets any easier. You didn't get caught up in that and did what you could to help, even though I asked you to stay put and observe." Ozzy's left eyebrow arched high.

I wondered if my intercepting Dillon McMasters was going to come back to bite me in the ass. "I heard every word you said, Ozzy, but there was something in me, some instinct I'd never felt before, that propelled me into action that night."

"I know. I saw the change come over you. Hal Rossi saw it too." Ozzy leaned forward. His large fingers steepled in front of his chin. "How closely have you been following news about The Scorcher?"

Okay, I wasn't expecting those words to come out of his mouth. I had disobeyed a direct order after all. "I've been keeping up with the fires on the news since I moved to Gloucester."

"That's what I thought." Ozzy nodded and sat back in his chair. It groaned under his weight.

I was at a total loss now. Where was he going with this conversation?

"I'm issuing you a department laptop. Tech support already assigned you login credentials. With this computer, you'll have access to the Gloucester EMS records. Fire. Police. EMT. 911."

If my eyes got any wider, they were going to fall out of my skull. I pinched my left thigh just to make sure this was really happening and wasn't some dream or fantasy coming to life. I felt the pinch. This was unbelievably real. I opened my mouth to say something, but I had no words for him.

"I can see you're stunned. Cut the shit. You're a good worker. I wouldn't be asking for your help if I didn't think you could handle this assignment."

"What is it you need me to do?" My heart was pounding in my chest and my hands were sweating. I hadn't been this excited about something since the first time Kennedy kissed me.

"I want you to read through all the reports in the system about these arson fires. You'll be able to access the incident reports for the medics and police through the fire records. You're going to be our expert on The Scorcher."

"I was always good at research." I was good at it, but I'd hated every second of it at BU. This was different. I had a vested interest now. Gloucester was my town. Ozzy and the members of the GFD were my family now. I would do anything in my power to protect them.

"I know." Ozzy's dark eyes glittered.

"You do?" My stomach flipped. How did he know?

"I got in touch with one of your professors. Turns out we go way back." Ozzy winked at me.

Jesus, my boss fucked one of my professors. That was one bit of news I really didn't need to hear at the moment. "What did he say?"

"Who says it's a he?" That twinkle was back. "Anyway, you're a stellar student when suitably motivated. Call me crazy, but I think working here with us has you motivated."

"You're not crazy. I love working here. I love my coworkers and what you all stand for."

Ozzy shook his head. "You stand for it too, kid."

I let those words sink in for a few seconds. I'd loved every moment of working at Firehouse Three. Even when I was washing the trucks or shining shoes, I'd loved every second of it. There were days when I wanted to come in and help out when I wasn't scheduled to work. For a screw up like me, that was saying a lot. "Thanks, Ozzy. I won't let you down."

"I know you won't." He leaned forward again. The chair creaked in protest. "There's one more thing."

Oh, shit. This was where he was going to ask me about Kennedy. How the fuck was I going to get out of this? "Sure." I'd tried to keep my voice level, but failed. I'd squeaked like a chipmunk.

"I want you coming out on fire calls with us."

"You do?" I couldn't breathe.

Ozzy nodded. "I need you to be my eyes and ears. Keep your eyes on what's going on with the fire, but more importantly, with what's going on in the crowd. Look at faces. Take pictures if you can. Listen to what the crowd is talking about."

"Arsonists like to watch things burn. Don't they?" I remembered reading that somewhere.

"They do. Listen to all of the 911 calls for the suspected Scorcher fires. I have a feeling he was the one who called 911 at the McMasters' scene. Learn his voice. See if you recognize it in the crowd. You've got your own turnout gear." Ozzy hooked a finger toward the lockers.

Without waiting for permission, I bolted from his office. All of the lockers were arranged alphabetically. I stopped at the last name Rossi. With deliberate slowness, I walked down the row of names until I came to one that took my breath away. Prince. Holy fucking shit.

I reached a hand out to trace over the letters of my name. A name, until now, that had stood for luxury car sales. Today was a new beginning for me. I could feel it in my bones.

"Try it on," a familiar voice urged from behind me.

When I looked over my shoulder, Hal Rossi was standing there with a smile on his face. His phone was in his hand, pointed at me as if he were ready to snap some pictures. I took the jacket off the hook and slipped into it. "Fits like a glove." I was all smiles. The shutter of Hal's iPhone clicked.

"Now the helmet," he urged.

The helmet was a thing of beauty. It was black with a shield on the front. Mine said R3 Prince. "What does the R3 stand for? Is that my droid name?"

Hal laughed. "Three is the firehouse classification and R stands for rookie."

I looked down the line at the other helmets. They were each numbered. "I still can't believe this." I held the helmet in front of me. Hal's camera clicked again. I was sure I had some kind of derpy lovesick look on my face. Finally, I stuck the helmet on my head and smiled for the camera.

I'd never been prouder of myself in my entire life. The first person I wanted to tell about this was Kennedy. Then Mandy and David.

Funny how I never once thought to send those pictures to my parents.

25

It was a rare night when all four of us weren't working. Ozzy had invited us over to his place out on Rocky Neck. He wanted to grill steaks and get drunk. I had no problem with either suggestion.

I'd gone shopping for the meat and potatoes. There was nothing I liked more than rib-eyes cooked over an open fire. There were no such things as cookouts or bonfires when I lived with my mother. It was rare she could afford steak and when she could, it was on sale because it was about to spoil. She'd throw it in a frying pan with some butter. We'd have French fries and some vegetable out of a can.

I'd nearly lost my mind the first time David grilled for us. I got to be his helper that night. The meat was red and fresh. I scrubbed the potatoes before piercing them and wrapping them in tinfoil. They looked like galactic Tootsie Rolls. He'd also let me season the meat and use the giant fork to set the steaks on the grill. My brothers stayed in the house with Mandy making a salad, while I learned everything there was to know about the art of cookouts.

Those were the moments that turned me into a man. Even though there were four, and sometimes five or six of us, David always took time with each kid to teach us things and to let us know how special we were.

When I pulled into Ozzy's driveway, I could smell the ocean. Next to grilling meat, the sea was my favorite scent. The others were already here. I could see Hennessey's Harley and Dallas' Stingray. I let myself in through the open front door. I could hear the others out back.

Rocky Neck was famous for being an artist's colony. There were still some shops open on this side of town, but the recession in 2008 hit the artists hard. A lot of them lost their businesses and their homes. That was how Ozzy had been able to buy this house with an incredible view of Gloucester Harbor and Ten Pound Light.

The little Cape had been run-down when he bought it. I can't remember how many weekends the four of us spent working on it. We'd installed wood floors and ripped out and remodeled the entire kitchen. The last thing we did was add the deck on the back. There was nothing better than spending the night listening to the sound of the gentle waves lapping the shore.

"The party can start now!" I announced, as I walked out onto the deck, loaded down with bags of groceries. I'd also brought fixings for smores. They were Ozzy's favorite. There was a fire roaring in the pit and I could see Hennessey's cooler filled with ice and bottles of his favorite IPA.

"It's about fucking time," Ozzy grumped. "We're starving. Where the hell you been?"

"We know where he's been," Dallas said in a knowing tone.

"You mean *who* he's been *in*!" Hennessey started to laugh.

I hadn't said a word about my night with Gunnar. He hadn't said a word either. It would have gotten back to me if he'd been telling tales. Ozzy had known about my plans with Gunnar. He must have been the one to spill the beans. My brothers knew that if I was taking someone out on a date, it was serious. I wasn't sure how much I wanted to talk about it with these three. I rolled my eyes instead of answering.

"Don't give us that shit." Hennessey popped the top on a beer and handed it to me. "We all know you went out with the kid."

"Actually," I said casually, taking a seat at the table. "I told Ozzy. I'm not sure how you two cretins found out." I pointed the neck of my bottle at Dallas and Hen.

"Good news travels fast, my brother." Dallas grinned. "We all know you were buttering that little virgin up, so he would open up to you."

"Christ, Dallas, you really are a caveman." I meant that. "I didn't take Gunnar out to dinner just so I could fuck him later." That happened to be an unexpected perk.

"Don't bullshit us, man." Ozzy was carrying a tinfoil lined tray with the potatoes on it. He slapped them down on the grill and shut the lid. "I saw that boy today. He was on cloud fucking nine."

"He was?" Shit, I hadn't meant to say that out loud.

"You've got it bad." Ozzy grinned at me from across the deck.

"What if I do?" I hadn't meant to say that out loud either. All three of my brothers were looking at me like I'd sprouted a second head.

"Okay, what if you do." Ozzy pulled out the chair next to mine and sat down. He sounded so much like David getting ready to examine a problem. "None of us would have an issue with that if you were sure it's what you want."

I hadn't expected to hear those words from Ozzy's lips. Looking around the table, Hen and Dallas were nodding too.

"Don't look so shocked." Dallas got up from the table for another beer. "Mom's always telling us that we weren't meant to live solitary lives. Maybe this is where you step off the bachelor path and see what kind of life you could have with Gunnar. I only met him for a minute the night we moved the bed, but Ozzy raves about the kid."

"I'll second that. Every time I talk to him about work, he's always telling me what a Godsend the kid has been." Hennessey grinned at me.

"Just because he's a hard worker doesn't mean he'll be a good..." I trailed off. A good what?

"Fuckbuddy?" Hennessey suggested.

"Boyfriend?" Dallas called out.

"Husband?" Ozzy said quietly.

I was at a loss. "Look, all I want to do is have a little fun. Can't blame me for that." Of course, that wasn't *all* I wanted.

Hen was shaking his head no. "If you can't be honest with yourself, then how are you going to be honest with him?"

My brother was making sense. "I like him. I can, uh, see myself with him, but I don't know what that looks like." Christ, I wasn't making any sense at all.

"Why are you being so hard on yourself?" Dallas looked like he had more to say but was choosing his words carefully.

"None of you are hooked up with anyone. You don't understand what this is like for me. What if..."

"What if you act like the asshole boyfriends your mother kept bringing home?" Ozzy walked to the grill to turn the potatoes. "What if you act like Dad?" I knew Ozzy purposely called him Dad instead of David.

That question hit me hard. It was my biggest fear. Yet another reason I ran from relationships before they got too serious. "I always thought that if I ended up acting like someone, it would be one of the dirtbags."

"Why?" Hen asked carefully. "You came to live with us when you were ten. That means you had ten years with motherfuckers and the last twenty years with Dad. Why would you think the bad you experienced would outweigh the good?"

Hennessey was making one hell of a good point. Again. "I guess it's been my defense mechanism. Every time I would start getting serious, I'd ask myself if this was when I would start acting like one of them."

"Maybe it's time to cut that shit and give Gunnar a *real* chance." Ozzy turned back to face me. "He's a good kid. Everyone at the station loves him. He's reliable and dependable. The guys confide in him and he with them. You know how hard it is to break into the brotherhood. Your boy did it seamlessly."

"He doesn't really talk a lot about work." Come to think of it, Gunnar didn't really talk a lot at all.

"Tonight might be a good time to let him lead with his good news." Ozzy waggled his eyebrows at me as if to say he knew something I didn't.

"Good news? What good news?" Gunnar had good news? Why hadn't he told me? Maybe because I hadn't been in touch with him since I'd left for work this morning without much more than a goodbye. Christ, I really was a dickhead.

"I'll leave that for him to tell you." Ozzy set a hand on my shoulder. "I know this is all new for you. It's all new for him too. Talk to Gunnar about your feelings and listen when he tells you about his."

Could I really do this? Be in a relationship? It was worth a try and Gunnar was the person I wanted to be with. "Yeah. I can do that." As soon as the words left my mouth, I felt lighter somehow.

The first thing I needed to do was call Gunnar and see if he'd had dinner yet. There was more than enough food to go around. I could chill with my brothers any time but this opportunity with Gunnar might not be available forever.

Digging my phone out of my pocket I punched the button for Gunnar's number and held my breath.

26

Gunnar

Kennedy had lost his mind. I was convinced of that after the bizarre two-minute phone call I just had with him. He started off by asking if I'd eaten, and then interrupted himself by asking if I was home, before interrupting himself again to apologize for the way he'd run out of the house this morning.

By the time we'd hung up, the only real information I'd gotten out of him was that he was coming over and bringing some kind of dinner. He'd said something about coming from Ozzy's house, so I knew that gave me a little bit more time than usual to prepare for his arrival.

I'd barely had enough time to brush my teeth and run a comb through my hair before the doorbell chimed. Kennedy didn't just ring it once, he rang it seven or eight times. It sounded like Quasimodo was ringing the bells of Notre Dame in my kitchen.

I don't know why, but I took my time walking toward the front door. Kennedy had been in a hurry to get out of the house this morning, and now here he was, twelve hours later, in a hurry to get back in. I wasn't going to make it so easy for him.

My entire day had been spent going back and forth about what happened last night in my mind. Half of the time I was over the moon, the other half I was panicking about what Kennedy's early morning disappearing act meant. I supposed his eagerness to see me now had to do with him realizing what a dick move it had been or he was coming over to tell me in person that last night was a mistake. If it was the latter, I couldn't imagine why he was asking me if I'd had dinner.

There was no time like the present to find out what the hell was going on with him. Taking one last deep breath, I opened the door. He looked out of breath and his blue eyes were wild with some emotion I couldn't quite put my finger on. "Hey." It wasn't the most eloquent thing I could've said in the moment, but I was still trying to figure out what the hell was going on with Kennedy and those eyes.

"Hey, yourself. I'm a total dick, so I brought you some food." He held up a bag and pushed past me into the townhouse.

I was still standing at the door wondering what the hell had just happened, when I heard dishes rattling in the kitchen. It was obvious Kennedy was settling in for a bit of a stay. I shut and locked the door before walking into the kitchen to see what the hell he was doing. He was pulling freshly grilled steaks out of a Tupperware container. "What is all of this?"

"Ozzy invited all of us over for dinner and some beers." With those words, Kennedy pulled two bottles out of the bag before reaching for what I guessed were potatoes wrapped in tin foil.

That was the first thing Kennedy had said so far that made any sense. "Okay, so you were at Ozzy's having a cookout. That I understand. What I don't understand, is how you ended up here."

Kennedy sat down hard. His eyes had gone from looking wild to wounded. "I had so much to do today, but instead of explaining all of that to you like I should have done, I was up and out the door before I could think better of it. I meant every word I said last night about wanting to see where things with you would go. I'm just not sure I know how to do that."

I sat down in the seat across the table from him and fiddled with the tin foil covering my potato. It was still hot, and I could smell the char on it. Dealing with the potato gave me a few seconds to myself to think over what he had just said. It made absolute sense. "I don't know how to do this either. Before you, I was with one guy and got caught in the act. Needless to say, he wasn't exactly all fired up to see me again after that. To make matters worse, I was too embarrassed to call and apologize." I finally managed to get the wrapping off the potato. I set it aside and looked up at Kennedy who wore a hopeful expression.

"The guys knew about what happened last night."

Kennedy didn't have to explain what he meant. "I suppose that's my fault. I was happier than usual at work today and Ozzy knew we had gone out together last night. He must have figured the rest out for himself. I suppose it shouldn't be a surprise that he told your other brothers."

"Good news travels fast, or some bullshit like that. They always like to one up each other with gossip, especially if it has to do with one of us." Kennedy rolled his eyes as if he'd had enough with his brothers.

Having been raised an only child, I had no idea what that was like. "What did they say?" I wasn't sure I wanted to know, but straightened my spine for his answer.

"You know Ozzy is crazy about you. All he ever does is talk about how much he loves working with you."

I was expecting to hear that from Ozzy. "What about Hennessey and Dallas?" I hadn't even met Hennessey and only met Dallas briefly. I couldn't imagine they had much of an opinion on me either way.

"They both want what's best for me. They always have. I guess it wasn't until today that I realized I wanted the same thing." Color rose high on Kennedy's cheeks. "I've never been anyone's boyfriend before."

"Neither have I." Is that what Kennedy wanted? Did he want to be my boyfriend? Did he want us to be a couple?

"Ozzy said you have some good news. He wouldn't tell me what it was, but would only say that I had to ask you."

Obviously, Kennedy was still all over the place. Were we a couple? Hell if I knew. What I did know, was what happened to me today. "Ozzy asked me to become an expert on The Scorcher. He wants me to read up on all of the reports filed about the arsons from the police, fire department, and EMS. He also wants me to ride along on every fire that could be connected to the arsonist."

Kennedy's mouth hung open. "That's an amazing promotion. How do you feel about it?"

"I'm pretty excited that your brother has this much confidence in me. Before I started working at the firehouse, I had no idea what direction my life was supposed to go in. The more time I spend around Ozzy and the others, I want my life to be spent helping other people."

"That deserves a toast." Kennedy popped the top off his bottle of beer and waited for me to do the same. "To you, Gunnar. You are one a million."

"Thank you." The words weren't exactly a ringing endorsement of undying love, but I would take it. I didn't even know if I was in love with Kennedy. I suppose it was asking too much for him to have figured it out for himself. I knocked our bottles together and took a long drink before I could spill the thoughts in my mind.

"I'm glad Ozzy left it for you to tell me, rather than hearing it from him. When do you start?"

"I got my department-issued laptop today. Hal Rossi spent the afternoon showing me how to read the various reports and how to access the 911 calls on the nights of the fires. What I was doing before you called was going through each of the arsons case-by-case and examining the documents and calls associated with each individual fire. Ozzy says a lot of arsonists like to watch the fires burn, so I'll be keeping an eye on the crowds that show up to watch fires in the future. I'll try to grab some pictures if I can."

"That sounds a little dangerous. If the arsonist is there and sees you taking photographs of the crowd, he could likely come after you." Concern marred Kennedy's handsome face.

I hadn't thought of it like that. A frisson of fear ran through my body. "I plan to take pictures on the sly, but I guess you make a good point. He could be watching all of us as well as watching the fire."

"That's exactly what I was thinking."

"Why do you think he's doing this?" It was the question that had been on the tip of my tongue since Kennedy first told me there was an arsonist praying on the city of Gloucester.

"I don't know. Some arsonists just like to see things burn, while others have a grudge to settle or a bone to pick with someone or some company. Since arsons in the Commonwealth of Massachusetts are usually investigated by the state fire marshal, it's not something we learned a lot about at the Academy. If I had to make a guess, this person started out with abandoned mill buildings and homes as a way to hone his craft, and now has moved on to residences where families live. I'm no psychiatrist, but it sounds to me as if he's escalating toward an endgame only he can see."

I didn't like the sound of that at all. "So, all of those earlier fires could have been a test run of sorts?"

"I think so. He was testing out different ways to start fires, how long it took things to burn. How long it took for the Gloucester Fire Department to respond. I have a feeling once you start digging into the research, you'll be the one to find these patterns." Kennedy wore a guarded look on his face.

"What is it? What aren't you telling me?"

An unexpected smile burst over his face. "I like you, kid. While I appreciate the promotion and extra responsibilities Ozzy is giving you, like I said earlier, this could also put you in the line of fire. No pun intended."

I had a feeling this was as close to an admission of his feelings for me as Kennedy was going to get right now. I could live with that. "I appreciate your concern. No one has ever cared about me the way that you do."

"I might not be very good at talking about my feelings, but don't mistake that for me not having any for you. Now that we've sort of worked things out between us, I'm anxious to see where things go."

So was I. "I'll drink to that." With a clink of our bottles of beer, the conversation was over. What I wanted most right now, was to dig into this ribeye.

27

"Spend the night with me," Gunnar whispered from behind me. I was drying the dishes he'd just washed. His arms wrapped around my middle and I felt his face rest against my back.

"What did you want to do if I say yes?" I slipped the plates into the cupboard before turning to face him. There were a few things I could think of to help pass the time.

"Oh, you know, I thought maybe we could play Scrabble." Gunnar poked me in the ribs before he started tugging my shirt up.

"Scrabble? You mean the game where you make words with wooden tiles?" I was going to play with wood, alright, but there wouldn't be a board game involved.

"Uh, huh." Gunnar managed to yank my shirt over my head. "You've already got a Triple Word Score waiting for me."

"I do?" I loved playing innocent like this.

"Right here." He cupped my package, giving it a gentle squeeze. Before I knew what was happening, he was unzipping my cargo shorts and pulling them down past my erection.

I'd gone commando tonight because I hadn't done any laundry. Can't say I regretted that move one bit when his thick lips enveloped me. His tongue toyed with my slit before he started sucking my head like a pacifier. "Slow down. Slow down. You're gonna make me come."

Gunnar smiled around his mouthful and took me deeper into his throat. He gagged as I hit the back of his throat. With tears leaking from his eyes, he lashed his tongue against my dick bringing me closer and closer to the edge.

If Gunnar didn't seem to mind going fast and furious, neither did I. My hands landed in his soft coppery hair, with my fingers digging in against his scalp. It was my turn now. Hitching my hips backward, I pulled myself back and nearly out of his mouth. Gunnar whimpered in response. I wasn't going anywhere. "You ready for me?"

His eyes widened. He moaned this time and nodded his head.

That was good enough for me. Digging my fingers a little more tightly against his head, I set a punishing pace, making sure my dick hit the back of his throat every third or fourth stroke. Gunnar's eyes stayed wide, glittering with unshed tears from my dick gagging him. His own hands clutched at my ass to help him keep his balance and stay upright instead of impaling himself on my cock.

Gunnar's sexy moans vibrating against my dick were bringing me closer and closer to exploding in his mouth. Drool escaped from the corners of his lips, making him look all the more sexy.

With my lower back tingling, I knew this was it. Feeling my come rise, I shouted out for Gunnar, whose green eyes had darkened to almost black. He wanted this as badly as I did. My dick twitched in his mouth before it started to spurt. Gunnar's eyes rolled shut. His throat worked overtime trying to keep up with my load. I slipped my cock out of his mouth and let the last few week spurts splash against his cheek and lips. Seeing him wear my mark like that was almost enough to get me ready for round two. I had absolutely no doubt there would be a round two.

With a blissed out look on his face, Gunnar fell backward landing on his ass. He carefully wiped the dregs of my release from his face, sticking his fingers in his mouth and moaning obscenely as he licked himself clean.

"Jesus, kid." I stumbled into the closest chair, still trying to catch my breath.

"You haven't seen anything yet." Gunnar yanked off his shirt, sliding a hand down his abs and over the sparse fur covering his abs. Within seconds, he was only wearing a pair of red briefs, and sporting a rather impressive bulge. "You know you want this." He palmed his package wearing a look that said he wanted to eat me whole.

He was right, I did want that, but I wasn't going to tell him just yet. I was curious to see what his next move would be. I didn't have long to wait.

Gunnar walked toward me and the chair I was sitting in. He slid into my lap, running his fingers over my shoulders and chest. "You're so fucking hot." He was nuzzling my neck while at the same time tweaking my nipples. My dick twitched and made a valiant effort to come back to life. It was going to take much more than this boy teasing me before I would be ready to go again.

To my surprise, Gunnar pushed off my lap and rearranged himself so that instead of sitting across my legs, he was now straddling me. This was more like it. I slid my legs open wider hoping for a little bit of friction.

After giving my collarbone a bit of a bite, Gunnar started rubbing his dick against mine. He was hard and hot against me. Like a gymnast, Gunnar went from sitting over my legs to standing between them. It was a move I never saw coming which put his dick against the side of my face. I could smell the musk of him and needed him in my mouth. Now.

"You like that, don't you? You're all rough and tough at work and sometimes you treat me like you're the boss, but secretly you like it when I take charge. When I put my dick in your face. When I make you suck it."

"Is that what you're doing? Making me suck your dick?" I mouthed over his erection, wetting the fabric with my tongue. It clung to him in all the right places. I wanted that hot meat in my mouth, but I was more curious to see what Gunnar was going to do next.

He rubbed his balls against my chin, before using his thumbs to slide his briefs down and over his cock. It sprang free and bumped against my nose and cheek before settling back against his stomach. That little move made my dick sit straight up.

Taking himself in hand, Gunnar rubbed his cock against my lips. Everything inside me wanted to slide my tongue between my lips for a taste of him or even better, open wide so he could stuff himself down my throat. He hadn't asked for any of those things, so I wasn't offering. If he wanted to be in charge, he was going to have to be in charge.

"Open up. Take a taste." Gunnar's eyes were glazed over, and I hadn't even touched him yet. I knew he was still riding high on sucking me off.

I wriggled my tongue against his slit. His skin was hot and dewy. Flicking kitten-like licks against his heated flesh, I felt him shiver against me.

"Now," Gunnar mumbled. "Take my cock."

"Yes, sir," I grinned up at him before obeying. I sucked him right down to the root, not giving him a chance to adjust or catch his breath.

Gunnar's hands grabbed the back of my head, holding me steady. Shoving his cock as deep into my mouth as he could, he stood still for a moment, letting me adjust to having him bumping the back of my throat. I gagged twice, the second time not nearly as bad as the first. I took shallow breaths through my nose. I could feel his dick get that little bit harder on my tongue. I knew how much this was exciting him.

There was one more thing that was guaranteed to push him over the edge. I brushed a dry finger against his hole. Gunnar stiffened against me, sending his dick that much further down my throat. He cried out, with his head tipping back, his eyes lifted toward the ceiling. I did it again and was rewarded with Gunnar's dick twitching and filling my mouth with his sweet cream.

Gunnar didn't call out my name or a sting of unintelligible curses, he stared down at me, his emerald eyes boring into my own sapphires. It wasn't until the last weak trickle dripped down my throat that he withdrew.

"Kennedy," he whispered.

I scooped him up in my arms, resting my head against his. I'd never had such explosive sex with anyone else in my life. Was that because Gunnar was nearly a decade younger than me? Or was it because I was falling in love with him?

28

Gunnar

It had been a boring night at the firehouse. Ozzy gave me shit about Kennedy leaving his cookout early to spend the night with me. I didn't tell him what happened. I didn't need to, if the knowing look on his face was anything to go on.

I washed all of the trucks, worked on inventory with Hal Rossi, and helped Ozzy with dinner. The captain had truly outdone himself this time. He'd slow roasted short ribs with pan-fried fingerling potatoes. I'd made the garden salad and helped cut the potatoes. My stomach had been grumbling for the last hour.

When it was finally time to eat, I started with the salad. I grabbed the tongs and set some in my bowl before handing it to Ozzy. I watched the short ribs pass around the table, helping myself to cornbread and potatoes in the meantime. Hal Rossi was passing me the tray when the worst thing possible happened. The fire alarm rang. "Motherfucker!" I muttered under my breath. I heard Ozzy chuckle behind me.

I slid down the fire pole, but it gave me no joy, at least not like it had when Ozzy had shown me how to use it last week for this exact situation. To be honest, I was too amped up to feel any kind of joy at all.

With as much speed as I had, I got into my turnout gear and boarded the engine. This would be the first fire I'd been on shift to assist with. As we drove to the site, I went over Ozzy's instructions in my head. Watch the crowd. Take pictures if I could. Be vigilant.

"It's another single-family residence." Ozzy's voice came over my headset. "Could be The Scorcher." The way he said the arsonist's name was "Scor-cha." It would have been hilarious to point out how he pronounced one R but not the other if we weren't speeding toward the scene of another fire.

As we drove with lights and sirens blaring, I couldn't help but think of Kennedy and how proud he was of me for getting this promotion. As happy for me as he'd been, he'd also warned me to be careful. The arsonist had an agenda and was likely to be more violent if someone tried to interfere with his plans before they'd been carried out to his satisfaction.

From where I was sitting, I spied an orange glow up ahead. I wasn't much for religion, but I whispered a prayer that the family who lived in the house had gotten out safely.

The house was fully engulfed when the fire engine pulled up. I stayed put, giving Ozzy and his team the time and space they needed to get their equipment out.

Ozzy hurried over to a huddled man and his wife. He spoke to them for a few seconds before waving me over.

"These are the homeowners," Ozzy shouted over the roar of the fire. "Everyone is out of the house. Find out what you can about how the fire started and if they saw anyone suspicious hanging around the neighborhood before it started." He didn't wait for my response, hurrying off to join his team.

"I'm Gunnar. What happened here tonight?" I pulled out my battered notebook, prepared to take notes.

"Jacob Metzger and this is my wife, Heidi. We were sleeping. The baby woke us up screaming."

It wasn't until Jacob mentioned a baby that I noticed the bundle in his wife's arms.

"She doesn't usually cry like that. Hope has always been a good baby, so I knew there was something wrong," Heidi swiped at the tears rolling down her face.

"You said the baby woke you up, not the smoke detector?" Come to think of it, as we stood here, I didn't hear one wailing.

"We only moved in a few months ago. What with the new baby, we didn't have the time…" Jacob trailed off. A guilty look replaced the terrified one in his eyes. He was realizing a couple of batteries could have been the difference between life and death.

"Did you see anyone in the neighborhood prior to the fire starting. You know, someone who didn't belong out here?"

The couple looked at each other and shrugged. "We had dinner, fed Hope, gave her a bath, and put her to bed. By the time she was down for the night, Heidi and I zoned out in front of the television. I can't even tell you what we watched.

Just as Ozzy suspected, a crowd had begun to form around us. I finished jotting down the notes from my conversation with the Metzgers. Before I approached the small group of people, I scanned the crowd. There were three men and four women. All dressed in robes or pajamas, with the exception of one man with a very familiar face. Standing at the back of the crowd was Dillon McMasters. What the hell was he doing here? Was he The Scorcher?

Butterflies rioted in my stomach. I wasn't quite sure how to approach him. It wasn't like I could say, "Fancy meeting you here." Taking a deep breath, I walked over to Dillon. "I didn't know you were staying in this neighborhood." It was the best I could do on short notice.

"I'm not staying here," he sneered. "I heard about the fire on the scanner and wanted to see if Ozzy and his crew were as inept at this fire as they'd been at the one that killed my family." Dillon was shouting now. Everyone gathered around was staring at him in horror.

Out of the corner of my eye, I saw Jacob Metzger approaching. Christ, this was all I needed, a fight breaking out at the scene of a fire.

"What's this all about?" Jacob shouted. "Who are you?"

All I was supposed to do was watch the crowd and take pictures, not referee a fight. "This isn't the time or the place, Mr. McMasters," I said quietly, hoping he'd take the hint.

"Oh? When is the time and place? My wife is dead! My girls are dead! When exactly are people going to listen to me?"

"I'm so sorry about what happened to your family, Dillon." I couldn't help noticing the reddish glow the fire was casting over his grief-stricken face.

A large crash sent a rush of sparks soaring into the night sky. It would have been gorgeous if it hadn't been caused by a house on fire. For one very disturbing moment, I could understand the beauty in the flames.

The seriousness of the situation crashed into me, in the form of the crowd backing up. The house was fully engulfed now. From where I was standing, I could see Chasten up on the ladder spraying water on the roof.

Someone knocked into me from behind, sending my body crashing into Dillon.

"You dirty son of a bitch!" he roared, swinging a fist in my direction.

I tried to back up, but another shove from the crowd propelled me toward Dillon. His fist smashed into my face and I could have sworn I heard my nose crack. I hit the ground flat on my ass, biting my tongue from the jolt.

I stood up carefully. Everything seemed to be in good working order, other than the pain in my nose. Christ, I hoped it wasn't broken. Dillon was charging at me again, shouting something I couldn't make out. The last thing I wanted to do was get into a street brawl with a widower, but I couldn't just stand here and let the man hit me like that again.

"Baby killer!" Dillon shouted, swinging his fist for the second time.

"That's enough, Mr. McMasters!" Kennedy grabbed the man's fist and swung him away from me.

Where the hell had Kennedy come from? One minute, Dillon was punching me in the face, and the next, Kennedy was swooping in like a knight on a white horse. As he dragged the screaming man away, I noticed the blue and white lights from his unmarked SUV. He must have heard the call for Firehouse Three come over the radio and had come to the scene. I assumed he was here to make sure nothing happened to me. For once, I was glad to have him hover over me like a daddy grizzly bear.

"What the hell is going on here?" Ozzy shouted from behind me.

Christ, here we go. It wasn't bad enough I'd been punched in the face and Kennedy had to rescue me like a kitten up a tree, now I needed to explain all of this to my boss. "Dillon McMasters showed up. He started shouting about us being baby killers and then he hit me."

Ozzy grabbed my chin, swinging it back and forth like he was a doctor assessing my condition. "You'll wake up with two black eyes. Have Rossi look at that nose to make sure it isn't broken." He dropped my chin and headed over to Kennedy who was casually leaning against the side of the SUV.

Could this night possibly get any worse?

I looked toward the house and saw the fire was out. Chasten was climbing down from the ladder. To my left were the Metzgers and their little girl. They were holding each other while the other firefighters searched for any remaining hot spots.

"Come with me." Hal Rossi grabbed my elbow from behind. "Rumor has it you caught one off the nose."

"Something like that," I muttered, following him back toward the ambulance. Shit! I hadn't even gotten any pictures of the crowd. "Dillon McMasters hit me."

"McMasters? Wasn't that man from the fire where…" Hal's eyes widened. "Jesus, do you think he set this fire?"

"That's what I'm afraid of." Maybe his own family had been the target all along. He could have set the other fires as a way of throwing investigators off his trail.

I needed to talk to Ozzy. After Hal had a look at my nose.

29

Kennedy

I didn't know who I was angrier at, Ozzy for giving Gunnar this ridiculous assignment or at the kid for taking it.

It had been a long night as it was. We'd been working on another honeypot sting, only with Ella recovering from her gunshot wound at home, I'd been working with a new officer. Jen had transferred into Vice after Ella's injury. She was short, with long blonde hair and a figure to die for. She also looked about ten years younger than her actual age, twenty-five. Jen was physically perfect to play the role, but I'd been having a hard time with the subtle nuance needed to pull off a performance that would make the potential johns offer her money.

As a result, we'd only arrested two men, and one of them was so drunk, he would have agreed to sell a kidney, if that's what we'd asked for.

My little detour to the fire on Hawthorne Way hadn't done much for the team's momentum. They'd all been ready to call it a night when I got back to the shitty motel out by the beach. All Mather and Welch wanted to talk about was the fire and Gunnar. I didn't know how they'd found out about our relationship, but I had a feeling it had to do with Ozzy's loose lips.

When I pulled into my driveway, I wanted a long, cold shower and to head to bed. Seeing every light in Gunnar's house blazing, changed my mind. I had a thing or two to say to him and he was going to listen to me.

With anger roiling in my gut, I stormed up his front steps and rang the bell. What the hell had he been thinking to incite Dillon McMasters like he'd done. Christ, the man was off his rocker. He could have had a gun.

"Hey, Kennedy!" Gunnar's usual smile was in place when he opened the door and saw it was me. What wasn't usual were his two black eyes.

"Jesus, kid. It looks like you went a few rounds with Conor McGregor."

"Feels like it too." He held the door open wider. "Come in. I was going to have a beer. Want one?"

A beer was probably the worst thing I could have at the moment considering how angry I was. "No. I don't want a beer. I want to talk to you about what happened tonight." My tone was a bit harsher than I'd intended.

Gunnar turned around with a stunned look on his face. "Okay, what do you want to talk about?" He took a seat on the couch, his hands folded neatly in his lap.

I sat across from him trying to get myself under control. "What the hell were you doing starting a fight with Dillon McMasters?"

"What?" Gunnar nearly launched himself out of his seat. "I didn't start a fight with him. He swung at me. I ended up on the pavement, flat on my ass."

"I saw you in his face, ready to punch him." I wasn't going to let Gunnar get away with playing innocent with me. Not outside the bedroom, anyway.

"That was after I'd stood up again." Gunnar shook his head. "Ozzy asked me to look through the crowd for the arsonist. I'd been talking to the people who owned the house that was on fire, when I noticed Dillon in the crowd."

"Why did you confront him? You could have just made note that he was at the fire scene." I was going to have a serious chat with my brother about giving Gunnar such a dangerous job.

"I didn't confront him. He recognized me and charged forward, yelling about how we'd killed his family but managed to save this one." The look in Gunnar's emerald eyes was haunted.

"Why did Ozzy give you this job in the first place? You need to tell him it's too dangerous." I was out of my seat and pacing around the small living room. "You need a different job and that's all there is to it."

"What?" Gunnar was out of his seat and charging toward me. "You were the one who got me the job at the firehouse in the first place.! How dare you come in here and tell me I have to give it up! Ozzy trusts me. He gave me this assignment because he thought I could handle it and I am."

"On your ass? Oh, yeah, Gunnar, you're handling it all right." I wasn't expecting him to come at me with fire in his eyes.

"The man lost his wife and children in a tragic arson. What the fuck was I supposed to do? Slug him before he could hit me? Jesus Christ, Kennedy, for someone who became a police officer to help people, you're acting like you have no empathy at all."

"Did it ever cross your mind that McMasters could be the arsonist? Why the fuck do you think he showed up at the fire last tonight? Gee, do you think maybe it had to do with the fact that he was the one who started it?"

"Yes, Detective Asshole, it did cross my mind." Gunnar's hands were fisted at his sides.

"You thought Dillon was the arsonist?" I wasn't convinced.

"I thought it was possible. He could have set the mill fires as dress rehearsals and the one with the old lady to throw investigators off track. I figured it was possible for him to have set the fire in his house to kill his family, but then I remembered something."

"What was that Sherlock Holmes?" Christ, I was acting like a complete and total dick.

Gunnar sat down hard on the edge of the sofa. His eyes had grown distant as if he were reliving the night of the fire. "The grief. That was the real deal."

"How would you know that? You were the one who had to stop him from contaminating the bodies."

"His wife and young daughters, Kennedy. They weren't bodies to him. They were his family. I know criminals can be good actors when the situation calls for it, but Dillon's grief was real that night, just like it was tonight. You would have seen it for yourself if you hadn't been so busy yanking him away from me and handcuffing him."

"So, I'm just supposed to let people go around beating up my man. Is that it?" I was yelling again.

"Why were you even at the fire?" Gunnar's eyes sharpened on me like a hawk, with me playing the role of mouse. "Police hadn't been dispatched to the scene."

Busted. "I heard the call come over the radio." I saw the crestfallen look on Gunnar's face. "Damn it, you can't blame me for wanting to keep you safe."

"I don't blame you for wanting me to be safe. I blame you for thinking that I don't have the ability to take care of myself."

"Oh really? This coming from the man who moved into this house with only the clothes on his back."

"That was a low blow, Kennedy. I get that you're angry because what you saw tonight at the fire scene scared you, but you just stepped way over the line. Get the hell out of my house. If you want your shit back, I'll leave it in your driveway."

"Gunnar, come on, I didn't mean-" Yes, I was over the line, but Gunnar wasn't listening to me.

"Out! Now!" He moved to the door holding it open.

"Fine." I headed toward the door. "I'll call you tomorrow after you've had a chance to calm down."

"Don't bother. Until you can get that condescending tone under control, I don't want to see or speak to you." Without another word, Gunnar slammed the door. I heard the bolt engage.

Using the rail, I walked down the stairs. As I stood in front of Gunnar's house, I watched as one by one, the lights went out.

There had been such a change in him over the last few weeks. He'd become more confident in himself. He'd made friends, hell, he'd managed to snag me and that was saying something.

Now, here I was standing outside his house after he'd kicked me out for being King Dick. Instead of showering together before bed, I was alone. Again.

What the hell had I done?

30

Gunnar

After the fight with Kennedy, the last place I expected to find myself was in the McCoy's kitchen eating my way through an entire Cuban Frittata. It was honestly the best thing I'd ever tasted. Topped with crispy cubed potatoes, the rest of the dish had scrambled eggs mixed with large cuts of slab bacon. I'd gone through several pieces of toast and half a bottle of orange juice. Nether Mandy nor David batted an eye over how much I ate. I supposed they wouldn't after having raised four very large sons.

When I finally set my fork down, Mandy's look turned serious. "We heard about what happened last night at the fire scene."

"Who told you? Ozzy or Kennedy?" I hated asking but knowing where the information came from would make a big difference on how much I told them.

"Actually, Dallas called first, and Ozzy called in the middle of the telling. I wanted to hear the story straight from the horse's mouth, so I hung up on Dallas to take the other call."

I snorted. "You hung up on one son to take a call from another?" I couldn't imagine sweet Mandy hanging up on anyone, not even telemarketers.

"I could tell by the tone in Ozzy's voice that there was something more going on than a simple man getting upset with you at a fire scene."

Shit and double shit. Kennedy must have talked to Ozzy about our fight last night. I felt myself sinking lower in my seat.

"It's okay, Gunnar. You can tell us what's going on." Mandy set a warm hand on my own.

If I hadn't eaten so damn much, I would have been able to run. Now that I was in a food coma, I was trapped. I had a feeling that had been Mandy's strategy all along. "Kennedy is a bossy son of a…" I trailed off not wanting to say the last word. "I hate to tell you both that, but he is."

Mandy snorted behind her hand. "I knew that the second day he was with us. The boys wanted to play a board game and Kennedy insisted on being in charge of everything. I think some people are born with bossy qualities."

David smirked at her from behind his glasses. "What has General Lynch done this time?" He snapped off a mock salute.

I felt much better knowing Kennedy's parents understood what I was up against. "He told me the other night he wanted to see where things went between the two of us. I'd never been so happy in my life until he dropped the hammer."

"What do you mean he dropped the hammer?" Mandy shot David a confused look.

"He was the one who told Ozzy I needed a job in the first place. Ozzy liked the work I was doing so well that he gave me a promotion. He needed someone to keep an eye out for suspicious people at potential arson scenes."

"Oz mentioned that the other day. Kept going on about how proud he was of you and your determination to succeed." David looked equally proud of me. A feeling I wasn't used to. I liked it.

"That's what he said as well. I'd asked to go on a ride along to a fire and for whatever reason Ozzy allowed it. It was that awful fire last week where a wife and two little girls died."

"The one where Ozzy got burned. You tried to rush into the house to help him, rumor has it."

I'd forgotten about that part of the story. "Kennedy held me back, but yeah, my first instinct had been to race into that building after him. Kennedy told me to stay put and had gone to Ozzy's side, along with the paramedics, when he came out of the fire carrying the little girls. That scene was the worst thing I'd ever witnessed in my life." When I thought about that night, I swear I could still smell the smoke. "The father, Dillon McMasters, tried to run to the bodies of his family when they were laid on the ground. I was the one who stopped him."

David set a hand on my shoulder. "I can't imagine what that must have been like for you." He turned to his wife. "I never understood our boys wanting to be the ones racing into dangerous situations, while everyone else ran the other way."

I was about to ask how Hennessey running a bar was running into danger, but bit my tongue. I had a feeling the answer to that question was none of my business.

"It sounds like you were born with that same instinct," David was saying.

"I'd never thought about it that way before. Ozzy said the same thing to me later, which is why I guess he thought I would be perfect for his little assignment."

"I'm guessing Kennedy thought otherwise?" Mandy was shaking her head in obvious annoyance.

"Not until last night. He'd been just as proud of me as everyone at the firehouse." It stung thinking about his harsh words last night. "He was upset with me for getting into a fight with Dillon McMasters who'd shown up at the fire shouting at the family who'd survived the fire and Ozzy. It was awful. A punch was thrown, and I was the recipient." I pointed to my two black eyes which had been covered by sunglasses when I'd arrived. David had asked me to take them off. To their credit, neither one of them asked what happened. Thinking about it now, Ozzy had probably filled them in.

"What exactly did Kennedy have to say?" David took a breath and held it. He was obviously bracing himself for the worst.

The last thing I was going to do was repeat those hurtful things word for word. It was bad enough they were still playing in my head on a loop. "He always feels the need to show up where I am to protect me like some guardian angel. Gunnar's guardian," I scoffed.

"That's our Kennedy." Mandy was nodding her head. "After what happened to his mother, he's always held tight to the people he loves."

"Kennedy doesn't love me." It just wasn't possible. "Love isn't telling me to quit my job. Or reminding me that I wouldn't have a house full of furniture without him."

"Damn," David muttered under his breath. "That's our Kennedy all right."

Mandy nodded at her husband. "Without saying too much, my son thinks that if he'd been stronger or braver that he would have been able to save his mother that awful night."

"He was ten!" I half-shouted. "I remember what I was like at ten. Skinny as a rail and so short that I could pass for a first grader. How the hell did Kennedy think he could have stopped a drunk and deranged man from stabbing his mother?"

"The same way you thought you could run into that fire and rescue Ozzy." Mandy said quietly. "We all play the what-if game. Kennedy's made it an art form over the years. We struggled the hardest with this issue when he was a little boy." David reached out for her hand, Mandy took it. "He used to run scenarios with me before bed. I'd go into their rooms and tuck them in. Kennedy had a new scenario for me every night for nearly a year. Broke my heart when he'd say, 'Mandy, what if I had…'"

I'd never heard anything like this before. I knew Kennedy thought he was responsible for his mother's death, but I had no idea he'd tortured himself like this.

"Now you see where he's coming from." David's attention turned back to me. "It's not that he doesn't trust you to do a good job, Gunnar, it's that he needs to be there to catch you if you fall, so there won't ever be any more what-ifs."

"I appreciate you telling me about Kennedy's past." It was true. I wasn't about to get this level of authenticity from the stubborn ass himself. "I guess my question now is how to get him to dial it back?"

"That's the million dollar question, isn't it?" Mandy reached for her coffee, taking a slow sip. "I think the only person who can answer it for you is Kennedy."

I knew Mandy was right, but still, I was hoping for an easy answer, a fairy godmother with a magic wand. "I'm still so mad at him."

"If I had to guess, I'd say you were more hurt than mad." Mandy's usual smile was back in place. "Let my stubborn son stew for a while. Let him come back to you. I'm sure he's hurting as badly as you are this morning."

"Worse, I'd guess, since he knows what he did to you was wrong," David added.

I had to admit that was some of the best advice I'd ever been given in my life. I couldn't imagine sitting at my parents' kitchen table and telling them about my man troubles. They'd probably come back with something about not having this same kind of trouble if I dated girls.

Looking at Mandy and David doing their best to help me out reminded me of a line I'd heard somewhere. Some people are born to be parents, for others, it's a simple matter of biology. My parents fell into the latter category for certain.

31

I was a wreck. After not sleeping all night and beating myself up over what I'd said to Gunnar, I was a complete disaster. There wasn't enough coffee in the world to get me though this day.

Gunnar hadn't called or texted. Why would he? I'd gone and ruined the best thing that had ever happened to me. My brothers were blowing up my phone. Of course they would after I had given Ozzy the abridged version of what happened last night.

Christ, how the hell was I going to set things right again? Not only had I told Gunnar he needed to quit his job, but I'd also told him he'd be living in an empty apartment without me. I really was the dumbest asshole breathing.

The question now was what to do next? I could pick up the phone and call him. Aside from texting, that would be the lamest thing I could do. FaceTime would be better. Gunnar would be able to see me and how sincere I was about apologizing. He'd also get a front row seat to how awful I looked. The sympathy vote never hurt.

What would I say? I'm sorry, was the easiest, but what I felt right now went so far past just a simple apology. I'd gone and questioned everything about Gunnar's new life.

I could picture him on the day we met with that big U-Haul truck and nothing in it. He'd looked like a man down on his luck, without a friend in the world. I'd been a dick to him that day too, but somehow, he'd managed to forgive me. Gunnar was the strong one. I tried to act all big and tough, but he was the one with real guts. I don't know what the hell I would have done if David and Mandy had kicked me out of their house. I might have started out as an orphaned foster child, but they'd quickly shown me the meaning of family. I know for a fact I wouldn't have recovered if they'd told me to leave.

Not only was Gunnar surviving, he'd been thriving. He'd gotten a shit job washing fire trucks and mopping floors. Not only had he taken it, but he'd managed to soar. Everyone at that firehouse loved him and I knew for a fact Hal Rossi wanted to date him.

Maybe that would be for the best. Hal was a good guy from a good family. He'd gone to school to get his paramedic certification and graduated at the top of his class. He volunteered at the local food bank and gave blood as often as he was able. Hal was the perfect man. He'd treat Gunnar right and wouldn't give him any macho bullshit like I'd done with him last night.

As much as I knew how good for Gunnar Hal would be, I wasn't going to give up that easily. There had to be something I could do that would show Gunnar how sorry I was and that I had all the faith in the world in him. Which brought me back to where I'd started. What the hell could I do?

I could go shopping for him. Buy him new clothes or a piece of jewelry. A nice ring or a fire department pendant. That might be nice, but on the other hand, it would also look like I was trying to buy his forgiveness. The last thing I wanted to do was solve this problem with money. His parents would do that very thing. I didn't want to remind him of those days.

Maybe a puppy or a kitten? Who didn't love animals? Maybe a sweet little dog would be just the thing so show him how much I trusted him. Christ, what if he was allergic to animals? I couldn't remember him saying he had any allergies, but dogs hadn't exactly come up in our conversations either. It would be worse to show up with a rescue dog and then have Gunnar not be able to keep it.

Shit, this making up business was harder than I thought. I'd never really had anyone in my life that I loved enough to make a grand gesture. Mandy maybe, but that was a different kind of love.

Yes, I was in love with Gunnar. I think I had been from the night he'd nearly burned down the house. He'd looked so lost and shocked by what happened. I'd wanted to pull him into my arms and tell him I wasn't going to let anything happen to him, but I didn't. I was a dick instead, insulting him and making him feel worse about the situation.

Speaking of my mother, I could call Mandy and ask for her opinion. She always knew how to make me feel better and I was positive she could help now. She'd know exactly what Gunnar would need. Only that was taking the easy way out. Gunnar was my man, or at least he used to be. I should be able to figure out what to say or do to get him back.

Grand gesture, then. What kind of gesture would show Gunnar how sorry I was for being a complete dick last night? Skywriting? Dedicating a song on the radio? Christ, those all sounded more lame than just calling to say, "I'm sorry."

Grabbing the keys, I headed out of the house, I was hoping that being out in the sunshine would help me get a better angle on this whole thing. I couldn't help noticing Gunnar's car was gone when I walked outside. I knew he had a shift at the firehouse today.

In the beginning, I just wanted him to have a job. Any job so that he could feed himself and be able to pay rent. I had no idea he was going to find his calling and make so many friends. In a way, he reminded me of myself when I went to live with the McCoys. I never imagined I would find a permanent home and a real family with strangers. Gunnar had a family. A well to do one and they threw him away like an empty pizza box. I bet he never would have guessed that by getting kicked out, he'd find where he truly belonged.

Now I'd gone and fucked that all up for him. Before I pulled out of the driveway, I dialed Ozzy's office number. I only wanted to speak to him if he was in his office and away from the others, namely, Gunnar.

"All hail, King Asshole," Ozzy's cheerful voice blasted through the cab of my truck.

"Hello to you too." Dickhead. He wasn't far off with his description of me.

"What can I do for you, little brother?" I could just tell Ozzy was wearing that shit-eating grin again.

"How's Gunnar?" I felt ridiculous asking my brother, like we were back in high school again and Oz had a class with my crush.

"Why don't you ask him for yourself?" His voice was smug.

"Jesus Christ, help a brother out here. I'm in over my head. How the hell do I apologize to him for being King Asshole?" I'd filled Ozzy in earlier on what had happened last night. He'd had no trouble telling me what a complete asshat I'd been, but what he'd failed to do was offer any advice.

"Why don't you start with just saying those two little words? They go a long way, you know."

"Yeah, I know. This was big, Oz. I really fucked up. I was sorry the minute the words flew out of my stupid mouth, but I was too proud to take them back." I took a ragged breath. "When I saw McMasters punch him in the face and Gunnar hit the ground, I swear my heart stopped."

Ozzy sighed. I knew I had him back in my corner. "I know where your heart and your head were last night, but what would have happened if you'd stayed with your team working on your sting?"

"Jesus, Ozzy-" I interrupted.

"Not *Jesus, Ozzy*. Answer the question. If you hadn't been there last night, what would have happened to Gunnar?"

"I don't know." That wasn't exactly true.

"Kennedy." Ozzy's voice had taken on a warning tone.

"He would have picked himself off the ground and made sure no one else got hurt. He probably would have gotten punched in the face again too. Or beaten to a bloody pulp by the mob of people. There. Happy?"

"No, I'm not happy. Neither are you." Ozzy paused. "There wasn't a mob of people there. Just some neighbors who'd turned out to see what they could do to help or to film the scene. From what I understand from the others there, Gunnar was doing a good job of defusing the situation until you rode in like Lancelot."

"Funny."

"No. It isn't funny. Look, I know that you're afraid something is going to happen to him if you don't hover like a tiger mom, but the truth of the matter is, that isn't going to happen. Hal and Max were on scene and so was Firehouse Two after we called a second alarm. Gunnar would have been fine."

"Okay, probably."

"Did you ever stop to think that he needs the opportunity to stand on his own two feet? It's part of the reason I gave him this assignment in the first place. I wanted him to see something through and gain some confidence for a job well done. He can't have that if you keep busting in like The Lone Ranger."

Ozzy had a slight point. Maybe. It was my turn to sigh. I'd been through years of therapy to break me of the thought that I could have done something to save my mother that night twenty years ago. It had helped a little, but not enough to keep me from repeating those past behaviors with Gunnar.

"You know I'm right."

"Yeah, I know you're right." He was. Ozzy always had my back.

"The kid is crazy for the lobster tail pastries at that Italian place over on Rodgers Street. Grab a dozen of them and some of their espressos to drop off here. The guys will be so busy grabbing the pastry and caffeine that no one will notice if you drag the kid off to apologize."

Why hadn't I thought of that? Gunnar had been talking about those pastries for the last week. "Good idea. Thanks, Ozzy. What would I do without you?"

"Drive our parents crazy. What else? While you're at it, grab some of those apple fritters too."

"Who likes apple fritters?" I didn't remember Gunnar mentioning them.

"I do! Consider them payment for a job well done. Bye."

Before I could respond, Ozzy was gone. He'd made some good suggestions. Things I would have thought of on my own if my heart didn't feel as if it were shriveling in my chest.

Turning the car toward downtown, I could only hope I wasn't too late.

32

Gunnar

In all the time I'd been working at the firehouse, I'd never wanted the bell *not* to ring so hard as I did today. I think I'd gotten about forty-five minutes sleep the whole night. Kennedy's aftershave lingered on my sheets and I kept waking up to reach for him, but of course he wasn't there.

Before I had to come to work, I must have picked up my phone a dozen times to call him. I set it back down every single time. Kennedy was the one who'd been insufferable, not me. He could damn well apologize. Besides, I didn't want to look weak in front of him. If Kennedy knew he could get away with *not* apologizing every time he acted like a first-class dick, then he'd always act like that.

After breakfast with Mandy and David, I half expected Kennedy to call me. I figured his parents would call and tell him what a jerk he'd been and that he'd best apologize to me as soon as possible. I'd spent the entire morning jumping at every sound thinking it was my phone ringing. It wasn't.

"How's it going?" Hal Rossi sat down next to me at the dining table. When we weren't eating meals on it or having team meetings, it was my workspace. I was about to listen to the 911 call from the Metzger fire.

I shrugged. "I'm doing the best I can with this assignment from Ozzy." I liked Hal. I wanted to spill my guts to him, but I knew that if this thing blew over with Kennedy, I didn't want there to be any tension between them over me.

"We all saw what happened last night with McMasters hitting you and Kennedy coming to your rescue." Hal sighed dreamily. "What I'd give for a man to be my guardian angel. Just make sure you let him know who's boss." He dropped me a wink.

That's exactly what I needed to do. Let Kennedy know who was boss. Me. It didn't matter that he'd been the one to start this. I was going to be the one who ended it. Reaching for my phone, I finally knew exactly what I was going to say to Kennedy. I was about to hit his number when I was interrupted by something going on downstairs.

"Hello, Firehouse Three!" a very familiar voice called. "Why don't you all come down here! I've got something for you!"

Carl and Max, who were watching *Die Hard* for what had to be the millionth time shot me a questioning look.

"I have no idea what's going on either." Shoving my phone back in my pocket, I headed toward the stairs where my suspicion about the voice was confirmed. It wasn't Kennedy standing in front of the ladder truck, it was Dillon McMasters. Christ, now what?

Dillon looked full of good cheer. He was dressed in baggy black pants with a Led Zeppelin tee and a casual suit jacket that looked to be a size too big for him. He must have really lost his mind if he thought that rag-tag outfit looked good on him. That's when it hit me that the clothes he was wearing were probably from the Red Cross. I'd heard they'd been helping him out after the fire.

"What are you doing here, Dillon?" Ozzy asked. He crossed his arms over his broad chest and pasted on a sympathetic look.

I didn't need psychic powers to know he was pissed at this invasion and was trying to candy-coat his anger, especially after what happened at the fire scene last night.

"Isn't this nice," Dillon snarled. "One big happy family. The gang's all here. Captain Graves. Hal and Maxine. Chasten. Carl. Jenks. Gunnar. All the people who let my family die. What a fucking moment. I feel like we need to commemorate this gathering somehow. Maybe we should take a selfie?"

"Look, Dillon," Ozzy's voice sounded strained as if his patience were only hanging on by a single thread. "We're all so very sorry about what happened to your family. I wish I could change the outcome. I really do."

"Change the outcome. Hmm, that sounds very giving of you." Dillion giggled. It was filled with nerves and something else I couldn't quite put my finger on. "How would you change the outcome? Hypothetically speaking, because of course nothing you do, or say you would have done, could ever bring back my beautiful girls. Suzi. Katy. Bella."

Ozzy tensed. He kept his eyes on Dillon the whole time. I was getting a really bad feeling about where this was going. My fingers itched to grab my phone and call Kennedy or 911.

"I'd give my life for theirs," Ozzy said sadly. "I wish there was more I could have done for them. The call came in too late. The fire was burning too hot. The point of origin was at the base of the stairs. By the time everyone woke up, Suzi and the girls were trapped upstairs by the fire and smoke. We did everything humanly possible to save you and them."

"Give your life for theirs? What a good idea." Dillon reached into his ill-fitting jacket and pulled out a gun. Without missing a beat, he pointed it at Ozzy and fired.

I hit the deck, landing flat on my stomach. I could smell burnt gunpowder as I lifted my head. Ozzy was down, clutching a hand against the left side of his chest. I could see blood pouring out through the wound.

Hal Rossi broke from where he was standing, running toward Ozzy. "It's okay, boss. You're going to be okay," he said in a calm, reassuring voice.

Chasten reached for his phone. The others looked poised to move and help Ozzy.

"No one move. Hands in the air. All of you. Even you, Superman." Dillon leveled the gun at Hal, whose hands were sticky with Ozzy's blood. "Now, one by one, I'm going down the line and taking your phones. We can't have the police showing up here before the fat lady sings, can we?"

What the hell was going on here? Was this some kind of hostage situation? Christ, why hadn't I called Kennedy. He would have known something was up if I'd been on the phone with him when Dillon arrived. Last night, I'd been so pissed off that he'd shown up at the fire to save me, now, I'd give anything for him to ride in on his white horse.

"Okay, Dillon, we'll do exactly what you say. My phone is in my back pocket." I don't know where that even came from. I needed to get his attention away from Hal and Ozzy, who was still flat on his back.

"Take it out and slide it across the floor." He pointed the gun at my head.

I wasn't about to play games with him. He'd been a deadeye shot with Ozzy. I had no doubt he'd do the same thing with me. With one hand still raised above my head, I fished out my phone and slid it across the concrete floor. It kicked up against Dillon's scuffed, second-hand boots.

"Now, you, Max!" The gun moved from me to Maxine.

Her hands shook as she did what he asked. She pushed the phone across the floor like I'd done, only it didn't move as far. Dillon walked up to it and stomped on it. The firehouse was filled with the sound of breaking glass and the gasps of the others.

One by one, Dillon collected the phones of everyone gathered around him. All the while a sadistic grin twisted his handsome features into something monstrous.

"Okay, you have our phones," I said carefully. "Now what?"

"Shut the bay doors." Dillon motioned the gun toward the three large bay doors opening the firehouse to the outdoors.

Getting to my feet slowly, I kept my hands in the air. My gaze passed over Ozzy who was breathing heavily. His eyes were wide open and focused on Dillon. Rage burned in his dark eyes.

"The buttons are back here." I motioned behind myself, but kept my eyes on Dillon and the gun he was pointing at me.

Dillon lurched forward, grabbing Max and pulling her to her feet. She let out a scared shriek. "No funny business or I'll shoot her. You know I will." The barrel of the gun was flush against her temple.

I knew he would. I didn't need to be told twice. Max looked terrified. She had a husband and two kids at home. There was no way I would do anything to jeopardize her or the others.

"It's going to rumble when I press the button. Don't be…" Be what? Scared? I didn't want to piss him off by accusing him of being anything. "Don't be surprised." It was the best I could do under the circumstances. My brain felt like it weighed a ton and information was passing practically in reverse.

"Just do it!" Dillon hissed.

With my hands held up on either side of my head, I walked to the control box and hit the button for the first door. I turned back to my captor watching him the whole time. When the machinery started to churn, Dillon jumped, just like I knew he would. That damned doors moving scared the shit out of me every time it started.

"The others! Close the other fucking doors!"

"You can only do one at a time." That was a lie. All five doors could be operated at once, but Dillon had no way of knowing that. I was trying to buy time just in case Kennedy or someone else who could help was on their way here. When the first door was down, I hit the button for the second. I swear it felt like time was standing still. I would swear on my life it had never taken this long for that door to close before. I did the same thing with buttons three and four. Last, I hit the fifth button. Our final lifeline to the outside world.

The temperature was in the high eighties again. Maybe someone would notice the fire doors were closed and would call 911. Shit, speaking of 911, what happened if there was a fire or a medical emergency? What the hell would Dillon do if the siren went off now? My stomach rumbled just thinking it.

"Get back over here. Down on the floor." Dillon was motioning me with his gun. At least this way it wasn't pointed at anyone.

I did what he asked.

"You," Dillon pointed the gun at Hal, who was holding his hands over Ozzy's chest wound. "Lock the side door. We don't want anyone interrupting our little reunion, now, do we?"

"I can't leave him. I'm keeping pressure on the wound." Hal wore a desperate look in his eyes.

"Suit yourself." Dillon fired again. There was a brief mist of blood before Hal's head snapped back and he fell to the floor.

The scream froze in my throat. Hal was staring up at the ceiling with a hole in his forehead. A puddle of blood began to pool around him. My sweet friend who'd accepted me from the moment I stepped foot in the firehouse. Hal was dead.

"You!" The gun swung back at me. "Lock the door. Don't make me ask you twice."

I practically ran to the door. My hands were shaking so badly I couldn't get a firm grip. It took three tries before the bolt turned. I got one last peek outside. There was no one out there. No dog walkers or joggers. The street was empty. I couldn't help wondering if that would be the last time I saw blue skies and sunshine on this side of heaven.

As I hurried back toward Dillon, I made a promise to myself that I would survive. Someone needed to tell the tale of what happened here today.

Just survive.

33

I did just what Ozzy said and went to the Italian bakery downtown. Mario's was a Gloucester landmark and had been my family's go-to bakery since we were kids. Every birthday party, Christmas morning, and special occasion weren't special without Mario and his works of art.

The pastry case was full. Great news for Mario's, bad news for me. I got a dozen lobster tails, half a dozen apple fritters for Ozzy, glazed donuts, which were Hal's favorite, a couple of sun-dried tomato bagels with vegetable cream cheese, and two thermoses of espresso. Lastly, I ordered fresh croissants, for breakfast tomorrow. After Gunnar accepted my apology, we were going to need fuel, that was for sure.

I'd wanted to call Gunnar while I was on my way to the firehouse, but I held off. I wanted my arrival to be a surprise. While I drove, I thought about the way I would apologize, without making excuses, and beg for a second chance. I only hoped he would give me one.

There was an odd stillness to the firehouse when I drove up. Not only were all five bay doors closed, the street was empty. In the middle of the summer, there should have been people everywhere, not to mention Gunnar shining the engines.

I parked down the street, not wanting to be in the way if the siren wailed. Something told me that wasn't going to happen. There was an odd calm all over the city today. My Spidey senses were tingling. Something wasn't right.

Certain I was just being ridiculous, I grabbed the pastries out of the truck and headed toward the side door. It wasn't really a side door. It was on the front of the firehouse, but they'd always called it the side door. I still couldn't figure out why the bay doors were closed. They were usually open all summer long unless there were storms coming in or it was after dark. So far as I knew there was no bad weather on the way.

It didn't matter. All I cared about right now was finding Gunnar and apologizing to within an inch of my life. I was about to grab the handle to the side door when a boom came from inside the firehouse. I would swear it was a gunshot. Why the fuck would someone be firing a gun in the firehouse? So far as I knew, there was only one gun on the property. Ozzy kept a shotgun in his office for emergencies. It was never loaded, just in there for a rainy day. I didn't know if he even had shells for it. The only other thing that could make that kind of sound was a flare gun, but again, who the hell would be shooting off flares inside the building?

Dropping the pastry, I duck-walked to the door. There were no other sounds coming from inside. Slowly I stood and looked in through the glass window. All I could see was one of the engines. I gave a slow pull on the handle and the door was locked. That door was *never* locked. Something very wrong was happening here.

I moved back to my truck and called my captain to let him know what was going on at the firehouse. He told me to stay put while he got SWAT and other officers on scene.

There was no way I was staying put. My brother and the man I loved were being held in the firehouse. I couldn't stand idly by and wait for SWAT and the hostage negotiation team. Since I'd taken my personal vehicle, that meant I had no protective gear. My bulletproof vest was in the department SUV and my gun was locked in the safe in my bedroom. I had a knife in the glovebox, but that wasn't going to get me anywhere. Not against someone who had a gun.

The only thing I had with me was my phone. Without thinking it through, I dialed Gunnar, praying he would answer. It sounded loud in the cab of the truck. One ring, then two, then three. My heart was hammering after the fourth ring. It was so loud, I could barely hear the fifth.

"Hello, lover boy!" an unfamiliar voice drawled.

"I was trying to reach Gunnar. I must have the wrong number." I knew I didn't have the wrong number. This was Gunnar's number but someone, probably the person holding the firehouse hostage had answered his phone.

"Don't play cute with me, Detective Lynch. I know damn well it's you and if you were half the detective this city thinks you are, you'd know who this was too."

I took a deep breath and tried to fall back on my training. I needed to treat this situation like any other case. "You're right, this is Kennedy." Who the hell was this guy? It had to be someone who hated Ozzy or the fire station enough to do something like this. Motherfucker. I knew exactly who this was. "Dillon McMasters."

"Give the man a fucking prize." Dillon laughed.

"Where's Gunnar?"

"Ah, a true romantic to the last. If I were you though, I'd be more interested in hearing about your brother and that paramedic."

My heart stopped beating in my chest. Ozzy! What the hell had this guy done to my brother. "Okay, how's Ozzy?"

"I shot him in the chest. He's bleeding all over the place. Looks like he's in bad shape. Not that I'd know. I'm an accountant, not a paramedic. Speaking of the paramedic, I believe his troubles are over." Dillon laughed again. It was high-pitched and made him sound as if he'd lost his mind.

"Which paramedic? Hal? Are you talking about Hal Rossi?" Jesus Christ, Hal was the nicest man I knew. What the hell had this fucker done to him?

"The one that was at my house that night. The one who stood by and refused to save my wife and daughters."

It was definitely Hal Rossi. All three of the McMasters women had been beyond saving when they were carried out of the burning house. Hal had checked their vital signs, but there hadn't been a need to start CPR. I wasn't about to tell Dillon that. "What about Gunnar?" I tried to keep my voice level but failed.

"He's fine, but he won't be unless you get the fuck out of here! No cops! I've got to get down to business."

The last thing I needed was for him to hang up. "There aren't any other cops here. It's just me. I brought pastries for Gunnar and the rest of the guys. Who else is in there with you?"

"The bitch paramedic and the firefighters who refused to save my family!" Dillon roared.

Going back in my mind, I remembered Chasten Coyne had been there along with Ozzy, but I couldn't remember anyone else. "Are they safe."

"For now. I'll tell you what I'm going to do, hot shot. I'll leave you on speaker phone so you can hear what's going on. If SWAT tries to breach this building, the first bullet goes into Gunnar's head. Got me?"

I got him. Loud and clear. "I love you, Gunnar." It was all I could think to say. When the chips were down and you might never speak to the man you loved again, all that mattered was how you felt.

"Well, isn't that sweet?" False joy dripped from every syllable. "What do you have to say to that Gunnar?"

"I-I love you too, Kennedy." His voice shook with fear.

Dillon's deranged laughter surrounded me. "This is better than I ever could have hoped for. I came here to kill everyone whose negligence killed my entire family. I never knew I would have the opportunity to return the favor. Say goodbye, Kennedy!"

Before I could react, a shot rang out. Gasps followed. Then the line went dead.

"Nooooo!" With numb hands, I tried the door handle. I needed to get out of this truck I needed to get to Gunnar. It might not be too late. "Gunnar!"

My hand slipped off the handle. When I tried again, I was able to yank on it, but the door didn't pop open. I felt like everything was slipping away. I was gripped in a wave of terror like I'd never known before. My panicked brain supposed this was what Dillon had felt the night of the fire.

That thought gave me pause and just enough calm to realize the truck was locked. I pressed the button and was about to try the handle again when the cavalry arrived. The street was swarmed with police cruisers, no lights or sirens.

Slipping my phone into my pocket, I climbed out of the truck praying that gunshot hadn't murdered the love of my life.

34

Gunnar

I felt the bullet whiz by my right cheek. That had been a near thing. With the marksmanship Dillon had showed earlier, I couldn't help but think he'd missed on purpose. Now that he had me and Kennedy by the balls, he was no doubt going to toy with us like a cat with a mouse.

The one thing I couldn't afford to lose at the moment was my calm head. Everyone's life could depend on what I did next. "Where did you learn to shoot?"

Dillon twitched. His eyes wore a look of shock. I guess he wasn't expecting me to still have my wits about me. "My father was a cop. He used to take me to the gun range. It was our thing."

Yeah, Dillon had definitely missed me on purpose. "Is he still alive?"

Dillon stiffened. "No, he's been gone for six months. Cancer. He was always so damn proud of me and my girls. At least he got to meet…"

At least he got to meet Bella, was what Dillon was going to say. I had no doubt. "I can't imagine he's very proud today."

Ozzy moaned weakly. I had a feeling he thought my words were going to get us all killed. I had a plan. I just wasn't sure if it was a good one.

"What?" The gun swung back to point at me.

"The reason I was at the fire that night was because I'd asked Ozzy if I could do a ride along. I was thinking of maybe going to the fire academy or something. My father isn't really in my life and I desperately wanted someone to be proud of me."

"What the fuck does that have to do with my father being proud of me?" Dillon's gun hand shook, where it had been steady before.

"Dillon, I can't imagine a worse tragedy than what happened to your family. Having some asshole upend your entire life for his own pleasure has to be the most evil thing I've ever seen in my life. I'm so sorry the ladder truck couldn't reach your family. I'm also sorry that Ozzy and Chasten couldn't get to them in time. They did everything they could to save your family."

"Don't you give me that line of bullshit!" Spittle flew from his lips as he screamed at me.

"Ozzy suffered a third degree burn and Chasten ended up in the hospital with heat stroke. They put their lives on the line to save you and your family."

Dillon was silent, but the gun was still pointed at me. "Your father is holding your girls tight. Don't make him watch you hurt anyone else. Don't make your wife and daughters see what your grief has done to you."

"You all did this to me and now you're paying for that."

"The only person who's paying is you, Dillon." As hard as it was, I tried not think about Ozzy being shot in the chest and Hal lying dead only a few feet away from me. "This is going to end at some point. You know that. SWAT is waiting for an opportunity to burst in here and take you out."

"Christ, kid," Ozzy muttered.

"Don't give them that chance," I pleaded. "Just put down the gun and we can end this without anyone else getting hurt."

"My life is over. I want them to kill me." Desperation had replaced the rage in his eyes.

"No, you don't." I gave my head a grave shake and took a step toward him. "I can see in your eyes how upset you are over what happened today. Don't make one of those cops out there shoot you. They'll never get over it."

"I can't live without my girls." I could sense Dillon's resolve starting to crack.

"Just hand me the gun." I'd moved to only a step away from him. I could see the pain and fear warring in Dillon's eyes. "It's going to be okay, just hand me the gun."

A lone tear slid down his cheek. "I'm sorry," Dillon whispered.

"I know you are." I reached out for the gun not knowing if he was going to hand it over or shoot me. To my relief, Dillon handed me the gun. "Thank you, Dillon, thank you so much."

Chasten was on his feet and moving toward the button to lift the bay doors. Maxine hurried over to Ozzy. More than anything, I wanted to run to Hal, but I stayed put knowing Kennedy and the SWAT team were going to race in at any moment.

"Gunnar!" Kennedy roared. I could hear his pounding steps as he ran toward me.

I backed up from Dillon, watching awestruck as members of the Gloucester PD swarmed him. Before he knew what was going on, he was face down on the concrete floor being handcuffed and read his rights.

Kennedy stopped short of me. "I need you to put down the gun, sweetheart." There was a tender look in his blue eyes.

Christ, I didn't realize I'd still been holding it. I set it on the floor and backed away. Kennedy grabbed me, pulling me into his arms. "I thought I'd lost you. When the shot rang out and the call disconnected, I…"

"I'm fine." All I wanted to do was hold him, but there were other concerns here. "Ozzy. Hal." I could barely get the words out.

Kennedy dashed toward his brother and the medics working on him. I could see there had been a sheet laid over Hal. It was too much. I sank to the floor and let my tears flow. I cried for Hal, the kindest friend I'd ever had. For Ozzy, who was fighting for his life. For Kennedy, who'd agonized over what happened to me and his brother. Maxine, Chasten, and the rest of the firehouse who'd been witness to the violence here today. Mandy and David, who might well lose a son before the day was over, and lastly for Dillon, who was undoubtedly going to spend the rest of his life paying for what he'd done today.

It never occurred to me until much later the one person I hadn't given any thought to was myself.

EPILOGUE

Two months later…

I finally had something to celebrate. It had been a long time coming, but good news was here at last.

The last two months had been a series of individual days. It was the only way to get through the heartbreak of what happened at the firehouse. Hal Rossi had been the best of all of us. His death was a blow Firehouse Three would never get over.

Thanks to blood donations from everyone from me to the mayor, and pure pigheadedness, Ozzy pulled through the surgery and his recovery. Hal's funeral had been held back for several days so that Ozzy would be recovered enough to be there.

The funeral had been the most tear-filled I'd ever been to in my life. Each eulogy had been sadder than the one before. Gunnar had been asked to speak and his words about Hal's gift for kindness nearly broke me, but that was before Tim Jefferson, Hal's best friend from childhood, got up to speak. There wasn't a dry eye in the house. It was true, only the good die young.

It had been hell trying to keep Ozzy from going back to the fire station. He was on medical leave and not able to work while he recovered from his gunshot wound, but there was this drive in him that pushed him to get back to his job. His family. He'd teamed up with Ella Gutierrez for physical therapy. The two of them pushed each other hard.

Today was finally the day for my brother. Gunnar and I had spent the morning getting the firehouse ready for a party. We'd debated back and forth about having a party in a place where one person had died, and Ozzy had barely survived. It had been my parents who decided the matter for us.

Mandy thought the only way to start the healing process was to make new memories at the firehouse. Welcoming Ozzy back was the first step.

I worked on decorations while Gunnar cooked up a storm with my mother. It warmed my heart the way the two of them had taken to each other, especially in light of the way his parents treated him after the shooting.

They never called Gunnar once. Of course, they'd done every media interview imaginable talking about how brave their son was and how they'd always known he was destined for greatness. Rumor had it the Princes were charging top dollar for these appearances, as if the two of them needed more money. I'd hoped they would donate that money to the Hal Rossi Fund or some other charitable organization like the Red Cross, but they'd kept every penny for themselves. I'm sure they would have called a press conference and had one of those giant checks made if they'd donated money.

It had been a long road for Gunnar. Not only was he dealing with the death of a friend and the trauma from seeing it happen in front of his eyes, he also had to face the cold hard truth that he was essentially an orphan. Mandy and David had been there for him through everything.

When it came to Dillon McMasters, he'd taken a plea deal, second degree murder with a sentence of thirty years to life. He'd wanted to spare the Rossi family the heartbreak of a trial. He and Gunnar had been exchanging letters. It seemed some of Hal's kindness had rubbed off on my Gunnar.

"He's here!" Chasten shouted, racing upstairs.

Gunnar ran over to me, threading our hands together. "My stomach is full of butterflies." He pressed a kiss to my cheek.

"Mine too." I meant it in more ways than one. Ozzy wasn't the only one in for a surprise tonight. I had one of my own.

My relationship with Gunnar had been the one thing that kept us both grounded. We'd managed to find a speed that was just right for the two of us. There were times where I spent the night holding him while he cried and others where he returned the favor.

"SURPRISE!" Everyone chorused when Ozzy reached the top of the stairs.

"Should you all really be shouting at a man who's recovering from a gunshot wound?" Ozzy's shit-eating grin glowed brighter than ever.

"Surprise!" the room chorused in a whisper.

"I can't believe you all did this for me." Ozzy made his way around the room passing out long hugs.

"No one deserves a huge welcome back more than you, big brother." I held Ozzy tight. I thought I'd gotten over giving my brother five-minute hugs, but apparently, I hadn't.

"Okay, boys, break it up." Mandy pulled Ozzy away from me. "When the two of you would fight as kids, I could barely get you to hug each other, now you won't let go." Mandy hugged her son tight.

"And here I was thinking I was the one with the surprise." Ozzy's smile lit up the room.

"Christ, you're not retiring, are you?" I snorted, hoping the rest of the room would laugh too. "I mean we went to all the trouble of throwing you this party."

"This is why I wanted a puppy instead of another brother." Ozzy looked up at the ceiling as if he were praying for divine intervention.

Mandy laughed politely behind her hand. "What's the surprise?"

Ozzy took a deep breath, his eyes had gone glassy. "I had a long talk last week with Bianca Rossi, Hal's mother. The GoFundMe page we set up in Hal's honor raised several million dollars. Once that Super Bowl MVP shared the link on his Twitter page, the donations poured in. Members of the other Boston sports teams chipped in and before we knew what was happening, the fund hit ten million dollars."

"I had no idea," Gunnar whispered to me.

"We discussed ways the money could be used to do the most good and Bianca suggested we set up a scholarship fund for first responders. Recipients of the fund can use the money to go to the police or fire academy, go for their paramedic certification or train to be a 911 dispatcher."

"I think that's a wonderful idea, Oz." Chasten started to applaud.

"We thought so too and I'm happy to announce the first recipient of the Hal Rossi First Responder Scholarship is Gunnar Prince."

I gasped, turning to Gunnar who was wearing an equally stunned look on his face.

"Don't look so shocked." Ozzy was smiling again. "You were the one who told me you'd gotten a call from the Gloucester Police Dispatch captain about coming onboard as a 911 operator."

"I just can't believe it." Gunnar sat down hard in the nearest chair.

"Believe it, kid. I know you'll make us all proud." Ozzy started to applaud.

"I will, I promise." Gunnar looked up at me, pride shining in his eyes. "I know joining Gloucester EMS can't bring back Hal, but I'll do my best to honor him every day."

"We know you will. That's why Bianca and I chose you." Ozzy swiped at his wet eyes. "Now that we've gotten all of these surprises out of the way, let's eat. I see Mom made my favorite meatloaf and pan-fried potatoes."

"Hold on just a sec, Captain Graves. I've got one last surprise." My heart was pounding like a jackhammer. I turned to Gunnar. "I've loved you since the day we met. You were bratty and I was, well, a giant dick."

"Cocktail wiener, more like!" Ozzy shouted out.

I rolled my eyes at my brother. "We've come a long way from that day to this one. I know I'm bossy and grumpy and hard to live with, but I promise to work on those things if you promise to love me forever." I dropped to one knee and held out the platinum band I'd picked out for Gunnar last week.

"Oh, my God!" Gunnar's mouth dropped open, his eyes stayed on me the whole time and never strayed to the pricey ring I was holding. His eyes darted around the room. My brothers had their arms wrapped around each other. My Mom was dabbing at tears while David filmed my proposal.

"Is that a yes? I didn't hear a yes in there." I hadn't thought it was possible for my heart to pound harder than it had a minute ago.

"I will love you forever, so long as you promise to always be my guardian." Gunnar set a hand on the side of my face. "Yes."

I could only hope my hands would stop shaking long enough to slip the ring on his finger. I kissed his hand when the ring was in place. I'd never loved anyone more in my life than Gunnar.

The room applauded in congratulations. Their hugs and well wishes could wait. I was holding my entire world in my arms.

From the moment we met until the day we would part, I was and always would be Gunnar's guardian.

THE END

Deacon's Defender, Book Two in the Protect and Serve series will be available this summer! Fire Captain Ozzy Graves is on the hunt for the arsonist, When a suspect is identified, Ozzy takes it upon himself to stick close. Maybe a little too close for comfort.

Have you met Psychic Tennyson Grimm and Cold Case Detective Ronan O'Mara?

Boston Police Detective Ronan O'Mara enlists the help of Salem psychic Tennyson Grimm to help solve the cold kidnapping case of five-year-old Michael Frye. Ronan, ever the skeptic, is out of leads and out of options. He very well could be out of a job if he fails to solve this case.

When the child's body is found, the work to identify his killer begins. As Ronan and Tennyson get closer to solving the crime, the initial attraction they feel for one another explodes into a passion neither man can contain.

Will working together to bring Michael's killer to justice seal their fledgling bond, or will unexpected revelations in the case tear them apart forever?

Check out book one in the Cold Case Psychic series!

Manufactured by Amazon.ca
Bolton, ON

14499416R00217